Hard Lessons

More Tales from

The Theological College
of
St. Van Helsing

Vanessa Knipe

BooksForABuck.com
April 2010

Hard Lessons

HARD LESSONS:
MORE TALES FROM THE THEOLOGICAL COLLEGE
OF ST. VAN HELSING

BooksForABuck.com

ISBN: 978-1-60215-113-0

Contents

Ashes of Memory

It was a punch in the gut seeing Simeon Carr pacing down the hillock into Carford Dingle. The shock broke Philip's stride and he stubbed his toe, nearly sprawling through the heather. He caught his balance at the last second and his running shoes pounded onto the stone path of the old trod, which ran through the moors here.

Following the slowest first year into the gully, Philip saw four other sixth formers waiting, standing by the school boundary stone.

Philip frowned. He'd read the literature, dug up by the new Headteacher, but this didn't look at all like the ritual described there. And Simeon's presence suggested this ceremony was based on the sort of thing that had got Philip's mother killed.

He wanted to stop, to turn back, to ignore this whole thing, but as a prefect at Carford House, he was forced to keep an eye out for the firsties on this cross-country run, making sure none of them got lost up on the moors.

Simeon was actively hiding his presence. Philip could tell when his gaze slid away. Like a bulldog, he shook his mind clear from the external influence. He'd seen that before the day his mother died.

Why hadn't they stopped her? Why had she been so stupid?

Then there was the traitor's voice that whispered, *because she didn't care.*

It didn't help Philip to know that the Church only pulled Simeon out of retirement for cases it thought were nothing. The man had been on that other hillside five years ago. Granted, Simeon had *tried* to stop the events--Philip hoped he was in better practice this time.

A grouse erupted from a stand of bracken, startled by Simeon's passage, and flew into the darkening sky.

That was all Philip needed--wet and complaining first years. At least the moors needed the rain, it had been weeks since even drizzle had fallen, let alone this promised drenching.

The first year stood laughing at the four sixth formers led by Head Boy, Alec. According to the pamphlet, each first year was to run the boundaries of the school and give a good wallop on a drum set at the boundary markers. Tradition said that Beating the Bounds would drive off evil spirits.

So what was with the pine branch Alec held? What was with the three drummers?

Alec laughing in the library--a place he rarely entered--gathered with his friends over old ledgers.

Philip's unease at seeing Simeon turned to terror.

Alec lifted his pine branch high, while the other three beat their drums.

'No!' He yelled his certainty into the wind that suddenly clawed down the gully. 'You mustn't do that! You need to stop!'

The wind pushed his words back into his mouth and tried to thrust him out of the gully. He fought back.

Alec saw his struggle, and laughed--a high gloating note carried on the wind, which combed fingers through the summer--dry grass and whistled through the upraised pine branch. It was last year's drop; Philip ducked the brown needles flying like darts towards his eyes.

He expected Alec to use the branch to give the first year a good thrashing. Listening to his half-brother cramming for the exams to follow Simeon into *that* branch of the Church, Philip had reluctantly absorbed old traditions. One of the original forms of *Beating the Bounds* had walked boys around their village boundaries and hitting them on the head at each marker stone. He knew of darker forms.

Instead, Alec held the branch high.

'No!' Philip shouted, but the wind caught the words and whisked them away once more. Deep inside him, Philip knew that Alec was wrong, though he couldn't say how he knew. He tried to take another step into the gully. Defeated, he cupped his hands to his mouth. 'Alec! That's the wrong way! Stop!'

Alec flung his head back, staring in ecstasy at the louring sky. Even over the wind beating at his ears, Philip heard Alec's words.

'Let there be blood on the boundary stone!'

The first year stopped laughing. Incredulously, he started to turn away from Alec who towered over him with the branch.

'Aaa-lec!' shouted Philip. 'Sim-e-on! Stop them!'

Slowly, Simeon turned to look up the hill.

Philip saw the lightning spike start to the sky to meet the fork darting down.

'No!' he shrieked. If only he knew how to push the lightning away! No! He would never learn that!

Oh-so-slowly, Simeon raised his hiking stick--his mouth moving at stop-motion speed.

The wind pressed against Philip's downward momentum, driving him back up the hill. Step by step he fought the wind with all his physical strength--and that wasn't enough.

Inch by inch the spike advanced.

Weighted down with millstones, Philip lifted his arms, trying to cover his head, trying to turn away. Down in the gully, Simeon leaned into a slow-motion sprint towards the boys. For the first time Alec saw the older man. He lowered the branch--as if he were using a wand to cast a spell.

And the spike touched the sky.

Lightning arcing down to strike his mother as the spell lurched out of her control. Her screams of pain, screams of terror from the other cult folk, filled Philip's ears.

Light exploded in the gully.

The wind stalled. Philip landed face first in the heather, buried under the sound of the thunderbolt. Heat ran over his back, scalding his neck.

He pushed his head up and squinted into the gully. The fire dried his eyes just looking. He thought he could see bodies lying on the ground. He'd heard of people stunned by lightning but surviving it. He had to get them out of there.

Scrambling to his feet, he tried to take a step forward but the heat from the fire pushed him back. He raised an arm to shield his face and tried again.

And Philip saw his mother reaching out burning arms to him, screaming in agony. Horrified, he turned away instead of trying to help her.

In the fire he saw a burning face; it looked like his mother. Horrified, he turned away. Screams sounded outside his head.

Hair blazing, Alec stalked out of the gully, carrying a now burning pine wand. His eyes burnt from within.

'There's Philip!' said Alec. 'Get him!' He lowered the burning pine until it pointed straight at Philip's chest.

Behind Alec, three burning figures stumbled out of the fire; their mouths open, screaming in pain.

Staring, Philip remembered his half-brother saying that the only way fire could control a human was to burn them, destroying them utterly. Where their feet planted, the bone-dry heather burst into flowers of flame. Burning arms raised and lowered, banging on the blazing drums.

Philip edged away, then turned and scrambled back up the last part of the hillock, using hands as well as feet. Screaming in pain, the burning drummers chased him.

Philip charged onto the open moor, heather lashed at his shins as his legs sprinted for the horizon. He cast a look over his shoulder while his feet kept pounding.

Behind him, three figures of fire spread out, carrying their deathly life with them. The widening fire began to play with thermals. It blew a wind straight towards Philip, driving the flames through the parched moorland.

'Philip!' shouted Alec. 'Come back here!'

Philip hoped the fire would be reported. Right now, however, he needed to run, hopeless though that seemed. The hot wind breathed on the back of his neck. He didn't think he could outrun this building wildfire.

They're following me aren't they?

Another glance back showed him the burning drummers herding the flames in his direction. Could he lead them round in a circle, so that the fire went onto already burned ground?

His legs fell into the regular stride he used for long distance running-- a very different one from the panicked sprint. He took a slight turn, but not enough that the fire creatures could cut him off.

Overhead, the clouds darkened further as smoke from the fire lifted and merged with them. Why wasn't it raining? Lightning flashed over the sky, but the promised rain refused to drop.

A check told him the fire creatures still followed. The main fire spawned little dancing devils.

Ahead was a fence--and a gate. Beside it stood a collection of fire brooms, but Philip knew the fire was too big to beat out.

As he vaulted the fence, a siren howled through the smoke. Relief. Someone had reported the blaze.

Running burned in his leg muscles--he was fit, but the ground was uneven. Fear of twisting an ankle in a rabbit hole concealed by heather added to his terror. If that happened then he was a goner.

He didn't want to burn. His mother had burnt when she lost control of the ritual using Philip's half-brother.

She only had you to marry your Dad, said the traitor's voice. To know your half-brother was properly brought up.

Bringing him up to save the world, by *magic*.

All Philip wanted to save was his own skin. Another slight turn, another glance--the fire and the creatures still gave chase.

Then his feet pounded on the trod. It went in the direction he wanted; he hoped it was a continuation of the path he had tripped over earlier. Running on the stone surface was easier--the path was open, not covered by vegetation. He could watch for uneven slabs.

Behind him, the fire was gaining ground.

Suddenly Philip realized the limitation of his plan. He staggered to a stop. Behind him the fire raged, but not enough time had elapsed for the older fire to die away. All around the trod, little fire devils sparked.

The main fire bore down on him, singing its triumph. Not a hundred meters away, he could see unburned ground and a road wide enough to be a firebreak. All he had to do was run through the fire ahead of him.

His mother screamed in agony as she burnt.

He took a step forwards. The fire reached hot little fingers for the uncovered flesh of his face and hands. He turned his mouth and nose away.

The winds driving the fire had come full circle. A huge, flaming tornado was forming--and he was at the center.

He was going to burn.

The flames leapt and clawed at the only way through. Why wasn't it raining?

Then Alec walked down the trod, his hair and arms blazing. 'Someone has to die today, Philip. And the man in the shadows stole away our chosen sacrifice.'

Philip backed away. 'It won't be me.'

'Blood must fall on the boundary stones.'

'The fire engines are here. They'll get the fire under control.'

'You put all your trust in technology, but what of the old powers, Philip?' Alec stepped forward.

Philip took another pace back; as the fire advanced on him, he could feel the heat from the old burn. 'There are no old powers.' He coughed as smoke wafted his way.

The spell out of control, his mother screaming as she burnt.

It should be raining. Particles from the smoke should be accreting the water droplets.

Seeing Philip's upward glance Alec said, 'We can stop the rain. The heat from the fire vortex evaporates any falling water. Stand still, please Philip.'

Alec took another step forward.

Philip's running shoes were melting to the stone trod.

'Alec, stop this! Let the rain fall,' pleaded Philip. *Please let it rain, so I don't have to burn.*

'I will only live as long as there is fire, you know,' said Alec.

Philip swallowed but his throat was dry from the run and the heat. 'Yes, I know.'

'Philip!' Another voice shouted. 'Come through!'

Philip risked looking behind. Simeon stood at the other end of the fiery corridor. On either side of the trod the fires burned, with heat enough to boil water, baking the pathway.

The Church people hadn't saved his mother.

'Philip!' shouted Simeon, over the crackling flames. 'I'm holding them off as best I can. Run through!'

It was only 100 meters. He could do 100 meters in seconds.

His mother had screamed as she had burnt.

'Philip!' shouted Simeon. 'I can't hold it back much longer!' He stood with his hands lifted over his head, palms out--the image of Moses parting the Red Sea.

They might not have saved his mother, but they had saved his half-brother from the altar.

Alec surged forwards and grabbed for Philip. Philip dodged.

I'm not going to burn.

'Stop him! He has to die,' shouted Alec. 'We must keep the flames alive.'

Philip leapt through the fire, kicking off his melting running shoes.

His bare feet pounded on the overheated stone of the trod. Ahead, he could see fire fighters whacking at the burning embers, as others unreeled their hose from the flame-red fire engine. He fixed his eyes on the dark, tarmac road.

And Philip ran.

Alec had gone silent. Philip didn't dare look behind.

The heated path wanted to burn his feet. He had to ignore the pain.

Why wouldn't it rain?

And Philip ran.

He saw the flame devil spawn off. Twisting and swirling through the air, it was driven towards Simeon.

A fire fighter knocked him out of the way. Another rushed to beat at the dehydrated heather.

No longer bound, the sea of flame rushed back to engulf the clear path on which Philip ran.

He heard the screaming. And the beating of drums.

His foot caught on an upraised slab and he sprawled onto the overheated stone. His hands blistered and he could feel his tracksuit bottoms starting to smolder.

A burning drummer leaned towards him. Hands dropping charcoal drumsticks, held together only by force of habit.

'Philip!' Alec's voice was a scream now. 'You've got to die. Please, stop the pain.'

'Release the clouds!' Philip said.

Four pairs of burning arms reached for him. But something held them back. He saw another face in the fire.

'Mother!' he whispered.

'Call the rain, Philip!' The crackle of the fire added the remembered impatience to her voice.

Why wouldn't it rain? Despite Alec's boasts even this heat couldn't evaporate all that water, it should melt the ice crystals sooner. This was science not magic--if he'd had any saliva left he would have spat the word. No! Not magic, which meant that it should be raining.

Mother's hold on the burning boys was slipping. Philip looked up. The long hose was just sprouting water.

'It will be too late,' whispered Mother. 'Call the rain or you will burn.'

'But you'll die if I put out the fire!'

The fire tutted, just like Mother. 'I'm already dead.'

The smoke crawled into his lungs and he coughed. And coughed harder.

Simeon shouted, 'Philip! Run!'

Burning arms reached out to embrace him.

It should be raining!

'RAIN!' screamed Philip.

The air filled with sound: rocks slamming into rocks in an avalanche, the din of demolishing a tower block. It drowned out his impassioned plea.

And then it rained.

The sky dropped the full load of water that Alec had been holding off--all at once. A lake of water landed on their heads.

Alec screamed in agony. The burning drummers were silenced as the water washed away their remaining ash.

Philip turned his hands over to feel the cool water on his blistered palms. Threatened with drowning now, he pushed up against the heavy load on his head and shoulders. He managed to get his feet on the ground and staggered upright. Water hissed off the overheated pavement. All around, the burning heather swam as the parched ground failed to absorb the sudden deluge.

It wasn't magic--he didn't do that mystic stuff. He'd been hallucinating from dehydration. There. That was the scientific reason for seeing his mother in fire.

He stumbled onto the unburning ground.

Simeon reached him as the first impact of water eased. He swung Philip up and carried him to the waiting ambulance.

A Warm Body for the Night

'It can't be a coincidence,' Josh said. 'That the Church's trouble shooters are invited to judge a Scarecrow Festival.'

Around them the trees whispered evening rumors.

'There's going to be a storm tonight,' Trewithick said, ignoring his apprentice. 'There's a Helm Bar.' His blond ponytail bobbed slightly as he nodded towards the peculiar bank of clouds building over Cross Fell. He slammed the van door and shrugged into his leather trench coat.

Josh dutifully studied the cloud formation hanging above the fell. The fell had been a bleak place to walk over; from below it didn't look much better. And that cloud which looked like it was endlessly rolling in from the West, held in place by the wind that blew from behind him. A wind from the East: that was never good.

'So, what are we doing here?' asked Josh, then remembered to add, 'sir.'

'Watch and learn, son.' Trewithick turned towards the village, indicating with a wave of his hand that Josh should fall into step with him.

They passed a tumbled down cottage that looked ideal for city-folk to convert into home, but had been left to crumble; brambles grew around the stones.

A woman walked up to join them.

'Are you Sir Nathaniel Trewithick?' said the woman. Auburn hair, with careful highlights, brushed her shoulders.

'That's correct,' Trewithick said. 'I must say I'm very pleased to be here and witness the resurrection of a Festival.'

'I'm Samantha Felters. I wrote to you after we looked up these sort of Festivals in your Encyclopædia,' said the woman. 'We needed help researching the actual words used.'

'A remarkable dedication,' Trewithick said.

'I wanted to update the wording but the older people, who remembered the last time it was performed before the war, wouldn't hear of it. And they won't join in. It's all so disheartening how these quaint village festivals die out.'

Josh studied the woman, who cast him a small glance. She wrinkled her nose slightly at his ancient anorak and untidy red hair. This was definitely green wellies and waxed jacket territory.

'This is Joshua Analay, one of my theology students at the University. We're really looking forward to judging your Scarecrows.'

'Pleased to meet you,' Samantha said. Her tight smile said otherwise; she warmed again as she turned back to Trewithick. 'And we've got a hog roast cooking in Fidlet's barn for after the dancing.'

'Ah! You don't hold with following the old ritual fully and have everyone staying in their houses for the hours of darkness?'

Samantha pursed her lips. 'We're trying to recall the good times--not the stupid superstitions of uneducated people.'

Trewithick lifted an eyebrow but only said, 'If you don't mind, Josh and I will examine your fine scarecrows.'

She waved them forwards, prepared to escort them.

'We don't want to interfere with your preparations,' Trewithick said.

She smiled and slowly walked to a group of people, looking over her shoulder frequently. Josh took note, in his head, on how to deal with pushy people.

Trewithick led him to the village green and they wandered around, staring at scarecrows.

'How fascinating,' Josh said, wrinkling his nose at the musty straw odor. 'Figures made out of rags to scare crows. You'd think they'd have a bit more imagination for a competition--maybe the odd cartoon character or a film robot made from a dustbin.'

Trewithick jolted down comments in a notebook. 'There's more happening here than eyesight alone shows you.'

'Isn't there always,' Josh said.

'Ah! The action starts.'

Men and women emerged from houses on either side of the village green; the women brought out trays and men carried boxes.

All the older people in the village skittered into their houses, hiding behind tightly drawn curtains.

So what is it that they know? thought Josh.

The men and women separated; mothers even handed male babies over to their fathers. The women huddled at one end of the Green, the men at the other end, arguing over who got the *privilege* of carting the boxes about.

Trewithick settled onto a bench. He folded his hands across his toned stomach and leaned back. 'Get what rest you can, it's going to be a long night.'

Josh sank onto the bench, next to Trewithick, who raised an eyebrow and nodded to the ground.

'It's wet,' Josh said, glancing down. 'Wouldn't it be better if I had some idea about what I was looking for.'

Trewithick frowned. 'Discipline is necessary in all that we do.'

12

'Pneumonia isn't,' Josh said.

Trewithick studied the green eyes that challenged his authority. 'You're worse than Dunkley when he first arrived. I'd just finished my apprenticeship, so I wasn't teaching then, but I heard he made life miserable for those who did--no wonder he picked up on you.'

Josh folded his arms and sighed. 'I prefer to be told what I'm looking at.'

Trewithick smiled blandly. 'This time you have to observe. Women's magic, men's magic.' He pointed to the two groups forming into parades. Among the women, Samantha led the group; among the men, one man in his prime jostled to the front. In both cases teenagers carried the trays and boxes.

Shadows drowned the village, while the sunlight lingered on the summit, like a bright island in a sea of night. Up on the Fell, wind blew over the shattered rocks, playing an eerie note, which carried down to the village.

As if this was a starter's gun, both groups started chanting. A woman walked from her house carrying a flaming torch. The lead man walked towards her and took a light for his brand from hers. Some from each of the groups gathered round. The acrid stench of kerosene drifted towards Trewithick and Josh.

With flaming torches lighting the way, they snaked towards the scarecrows that guarded each of the houses and stood around the Green. Josh began to hear the words they were singing.

What are little babies made of, made of?
What are little babies made of?
Nappies and crumbs and sucking their thumbs,
That's what little babies are made of?

Josh snickered. 'Nursery rhymes?'

'You know everything, of course,' Trewithick said.

Josh shrugged and turned back to the groups. Each had reached a group of scarecrows. From the trays and boxes nappies appeared to clothe strawbabies, while others sprinkled crumbs or bent arms, so that the smallest figures appeared to be sucking their thumbs.

The eerie shriek like haunted souls whistled down the valley; Josh felt the hairs on the back of his neck rising. He jerked his head back to Trewithick who lifted a finger to his lips. The wind whipped the flames from the torches. Over the howl he could hear bass chanting from the men.

What are little boys made of, made of?

What are little boys made of?
Frogs and snails and puppy-dog tails,
That's what little boys are made of.

'Puppy dogs tails?' Josh burst out.

Trewithick smiled. 'Ah! You do have something to learn after all. Samantha contacted me when she realized it was illegal to dock the tails of dogs. I helped her discover a legal and theologically appropriate alternative--knotted rope. Now hush, you could ruin it all with a misplaced word.'

Josh saw the men reach into their boxes and begin distributing snails and frogs over some of the straw figures. Ends of rope were knotted onto the arms and legs.

The women took over the chanting as they reached onto their trays.

What are little girls made of, made of?
What are little girls made of?
Sugar and spice and all things nice,
That's what little girls are made of.

The light that lingered on the summit began to shed sparks, which drifted down from the Fell as if the wind had blown stars from the sky. Josh caught on that he was seeing nature spirits coming down from the hills. Everywhere he looked, the lights drifted towards the village. Trewithick watched too; the fading twilight turned his blond hair to silver--almost like he would dissolve into a spirit light himself.

Trewithick stretched and tucked his arms behind his head. As if he had just remembered his apprentice's presence Trewithick said, 'The old people round here would call them the souls of the people the hills have taken for sacrifice when humans stopped offering them their due.'

The men took over the chant.

What are young men made of, made of?
What are young men made of?
Sighs and leers and crocodile tears,
That's what young men are made of.

Two teenaged boys self-consciously performed a ritual fight. Teenage girls giggled behind their hands.

I'd feel a right prat doing that in front of those girls, thought Josh. The older men dripped water onto some of the straw figures.

Now that all the groups of scarecrows on the Green had been visited the groups of men and women split into smaller groups to visit the houses.

The women sang now.

What are young women made of, made of?
What are young women made of?
Ribbons and rings and other fine things,
That's what young women are made of.

At each stop the scarecrows were adorned with appropriate symbols.

With the torches scattered all over the village, Josh and Trewithick were in almost darkness--except for the soul lights pulled down from the hills. The howling wind was building.

'Did you know that Cross Fell is also called Fiend's Fell?' breathed Trewithick.

Tormented souls in Hell couldn't have made such a racket. Josh grimaced.

What are our fathers made of, made of?
What are our fathers made of?
Pipes and smoke and collars that choke,
That's what our fathers are made of.

From the shadows Trewithick spoke again. 'The villagers used to say this was the only way to placate the dead souls--of course no one believes in it now.'

What are our mothers made of, made of?
What are our mothers made of?
Aprons and cases and sweet pretty faces;
That's what our mothers are made of.

What are old men made of, made of?
What are old men made of?
Slippers that flop and a bald-headed top;
That's what old men are made of.

What are old women made of, made of?
What are old women made of?
Knitting and reels and old spinning wheels;
That's what old women are made of?

Josh felt the hills pushing down on him. The air was too heavy to breathe and all the while he could see, in the last reflected light of sunset, the coiling cloud, waiting above the Fell to roll down on the village.

The scattered groups gathered on the village green again. They flung their torches to form a bonfire. Then the men and women joined lines facing each other.

Out on the green, musicians started a dance tune and men ran across to the waiting line of women. Each man and boy grabbed a woman or girl from the line and danced a wild reel. Laughter reached where Trewithick and Josh sat on the bench. Josh felt an easing of the pressure that had been building throughout the ritual.

He breathed again. 'Can't we go and join them, now they're finished. That looks fun.'

Trewithick shook his head. 'We are here to observe that the rituals take place correctly, and to advise if the rituals need changing. This is a Village thing. Look to the hills.'

Josh strained to look beyond the lighted village green and even more soul lights crowded the edge of the village, pushing at the light.

The music took on frenzied pace and the dancers stumbled to keep time. One couple danced up to the bonfire and kicked brands from the heap. To wild cheering from the rest they trampled the flames. Then another couple and another, until one by one, the lights were stamped out.

Shadows crawled over the tops; true dark crept up on them. Dusk had failed to turn on the orange streetlights, which stood around the village.

As the last flame was crushed under booted feet, the East Wind died. The music stopped, mid-phrase. Calm dropped over the Green. No longer held back by the East Wind, the Helm Bar cloud rolled towards the village.

And blown out of the hills, before the huge cloud, came the ghost lights.

They drifted down the street and between the houses, seeking something. Josh watched as one stopped, then it sank into a scarecrow.

The straw figure stood up.

Everywhere he looked he saw soul lights fading into the straw figures.

Unseeing, the laughing men wrestled women into an armlock and manhandled them off the Village Green and towards a brightly lit barn. In some cases, to Josh's amusement, a little girl frogmarched a little boy, who hadn't yet caught on to misogyny. The protests were loud and ritualized.

What are all people made of, made of?
What are all people made of?
Fighting a spot and loving a lot,
That's what all people are made of.

Trewithick stood and fastened his trenchcoat. Josh hugged his anorak closer. The night was getting cold.

'Shouldn't we be going inside, sir?' Josh asked.

Trewithick shook his head, the soul lights making his blue eyes brilliant. 'We must observe.'

Josh held his breath. Were the villagers going to get to the barn before they noticed walking scarecrows?

'Sir!' He turned and saw Trewithick's face had that marble angel cast that told Josh that he was performing a working. Josh bit his tongue.

Trewithick glanced at his apprentice. His smile was distant; it failed to reach those brilliant eyes. 'I can't hold back the storm. Tonight will be... frenetic. All of their *life* lived in one Night.'

The wind dived down from the Fell, pushing the rain before it. A squall soaked Josh's jeans. He understood now why the older apprentices all had long raincoats.

He squinted through the rain and saw laughing people running for shelter. Maybe they'd get inside before the storm broke fully.

He turned his face away from where the wind tried to steal every breath. Trewithick grabbed his arm and leant in to shout. 'I hoped my alteration would be enough to stop this happening but they are desperate for the chance to *live*. Back to the van. You'll need a better coat to last this night.'

Bent over like a turtle, Josh followed Trewithick back along the road to where they had parked the van.

All around them, the straw people stood up as they absorbed the soul lights. The wind had no effect on them. They shambled along like puppets, taking no notice of two men out in the dark.

Once at the van, Trewithick produced an ankle-length plastic rain mac, which Josh gratefully hauled over his anorak and fastened it shut with the belt. He was about to shout his thanks to Trewithick when a girl screamed in the darkness.

Wild eyed, Trewithick dived into the back of his van. He backed out holding his cane and a long sword. He tossed the sword to Josh who caught it by the hilt. It felt like warm ice in his hand.

'Hope you've been paying attention in the Ancient Gym class. You'll need it tonight,' Trewithick said grimly.

Josh nodded, distracted by the energies of the night thrumming through the blade. Trewithick slammed the doors on his van and pulled out a second blade hidden inside his cane.

'Come on,' he shouted, charging into the night.

Even with the wind behind him, Josh struggled to keep up with his teacher. Josh marveled that Trewithick was over forty.

Trewithick slowed. Holding his head close to Josh's ear he said, 'We need to get everyone behind locked doors to be safe for the night--especially the women. Tell them not to open the door again once it is locked.'

'But the scarecrows aren't doing anything.'

'Not yet,' Trewithick said. 'Do you know the story of the demon's egg?'

Josh shook his head.

'Look it up when we get back to college. Suffice to say we do not want one of these spirit creatures... implanting a baby in a woman. Split up. Don't let one of the creatures even touch a woman.'

He ran into the dark. Josh trotted the other way. He immediately found a group of people running around like leaves in the wind.

'Get into your houses,' he shouted. The people saw a man with a sword--it should have added to their terror, but they seemed reassured someone was taking command.

The father picked up his daughter and grabbed the boy's hand and fled towards a house. Josh ran with them. A scarecrow stood at the gate. The little girl screamed. Josh sprinted ahead. He slashed at the ambling creature, cutting it into pieces. The rags fell to the ground, spilling their straw. The wind seized the damp straw and flung it into Josh's face. Holding the gate open, he sneezed as the musty smell got up his nose. The man charged his family through.

Josh saw them all inside. 'Don't open the door once it's locked. Not for anything.'

Though lightning flashes Josh saw Trewithick had organized most of the people into the barn. Men pulled the door closed. The Green was nearly clear. Josh dashed off and got another young family inside.

'But my wife,' the man objected when told not to open the door again tonight, 'She's still out in this. It's a dreadful storm.'

'I'll get her to safety,' Josh said. 'She's probably in the barn.'

The man looked relieved. 'Of course, she was doing all the organizing. She'd be in before the rest of them.' He retreated indoors, determined not to see odd things happening in the night.

Squinting through the worsening weather, Josh spotted Trewithick. The Green was clear of people. Trewithick stood in the centre of the Green holding his hands to the sky in a pose of appeal.

Josh trotted towards him.

Energies prickled the hairs on the back of his neck. Recognizing a major working, he ducked into the bus shelter. Sheltered from the pounding rain, he propped the sword against the wall and pushed the hood off. He tucked his ginger hair behind his ears, regretting that it hadn't yet grown long enough for the trademark college ponytail.

Trewithick lowered his hands and ran into the shelter. His coat had no hood. He wiped his face clear of rain.

'I'm going to get one of those umbrella hats,' he said. 'You did tell them not to open their doors again tonight?'

'Yes,' Josh said. 'What do we do now?'

'You mean do we have to go back out in that, do you?'

'Actually I did,' Josh said, grinning.

'We need to rebalance the energies around here, but I'm sure...'

A female scream sounded through the thunder.

Trewithick swore. 'We didn't get them all. Come on.'

He wrenched the sword out from his cane again.

Snatching up the borrowed sword, Josh sprinted after him with the rain lashing his face, wondering just how he was supposed to find some silly bint in this dark.

The scream sounded again. This time closer and more terrified. He scrambled over a wall into a garden and found the girl huddled against a shed with a scarecrow looming over her.

Trewithick vaulted the back wall. He ploughed straight into the scarecrow. He sliced the head off and hacked away an arm with the back swing. The creature lurched another step towards the girl.

Josh took a double-handed swipe from neck to groin. The creature fell in two.

Then all the parts started inching towards her.

Blinking raindrops from his lashes, Josh hacked at the piece nearest her foot. She screamed again.

'Shut up!' shouted Trewithick, kicking at a scarecrow arm.

The girl stared at him, her white face indistinct through the rain. She opened her mouth, but Trewithick slapped her across the cheek with his left hand--the free one.

'I said shut up,' he shouted over the howling wind. 'You'll bring more of them down on us.'

Josh chopped at the ground and stomping frantically, trying to kill the bits of straw that shouldn't even be alive. Then the wind caught the fragments and hauled them into the sky.

Panting, Josh lowered the sword. More scarecrows leaned against the back wall.

'If enough of them get here, they'll push that wall over,' he shouted to his tutor.

Trewithick looked around for escape. He grabbed the girl roughly by the wrist and jerked her to her feet.

'We'll have to put her in the van for the night,' he shouted back.

'We'll never get her through this lot,' Josh said. 'Let's just knock on a door and post her into that house.'

Trewithick shook his head. Strands of hair had come lose from his tidy ponytail and plastered over his face.

'If anyone opens a door tonight, it will give all creatures a standing invitation to enter, for all eternity. Why do you think there are abandoned cottages in this village?'

Josh looked where the scarecrows leered over the wall. 'Think we can get out of the front?'

The girl buried her face in her hands.

'Get ready to run,' Trewithick shouted.

Josh nodded but looked doubtfully at the girl. Trewithick grinned. In one swift motion like a shrug, he hoisted the girl over his left shoulder, holding her on carefully, and non-controversially, over her knees. With an indignant gasp the girl battered his shoulder with a fist.

'Put me down!'

'Stop struggling please.'

Josh put his face up to the girl's ear. 'If you don't quit moving about, you're in the perfect position for him to give you a right hiding, so you can't sit for a week.'

She said something, but Trewithick's coat and the storm muffled it.

'So I'd lie still if I were you,' continued Josh.

'Thank you, Josh,' Trewithick said.

But the girl lay still.

'Lead the way will you, son?' Trewithick said.

Josh nodded.

Holding the sword down he crept around the house.

The scarecrows began to shamble from the back wall to follow them. Josh upped the pace.

Three scarecrows hovered by the front gate, not as many as at the back wall. He turned to report this to Trewithick, but the man was behind him.

'They don't feel pain,' whispered Trewithick in his ear. 'You have to chop them to pieces.'

'Okay!'

'I hate to ask this of you, but stay between them and the girl. It is vital that none of them touch the girl.'

'This umm... implanting doesn't happen the normal way, then?'

'Not quite,' Trewithick said, wryly. 'They don't have the equipment.'

Josh spat some wet hair from his mouth. 'If we're going...'

He charged over to the gate and kicked it open, knocking two of the scarecrows over. While they tried to rise, he slashed at the third until the wind whipped away the remains. Trewithick slid past him, holding his own sword at ready.

Having dealt with one Josh backed up rapidly to keep up with Trewithick's steady jog.

'Josh! Josh! Where are you?'

Josh lowered his sword. 'Mum is that you?'

His Mum sounded really worried. He really shouldn't be hiding from her like this. Guilt drove Josh into the garden from behind the buddleia.

'It's okay Mum, I was just playing hide and seek with the Carter boys.'

Mum stood with hands on hips. 'How many times do I have to tell you not to play with those rough boys.'

'But Mum.' Josh could hear the whine creep into his voice. 'They're the only kids my age.'

'And their Dad beats them up. I didn't go through all the hassle of divorcing your foul father, to have you fall under the influence of another bruiser...'

There was a crash of metal that sounded like someone had dropped a pan lid. Vibrations quivered through the sword in his hand. What was he doing carrying something like that? His Mum would hate him playing with a sword.

Trewithick clashed his blade again, with the flat of his sword.

'Where's Mum? I...' Josh looked around. 'Umm sorry. I...'

'They're starting to tempt you from your post,' Trewithick said. 'You're doing better than average, for a first year, but be wary.'

Josh took a firmer grip on the rain-slick sword hilt. 'Yes, Sir!'

He darted glances into the indistinct gardens, wishing that there were streetlights here. He walked backwards, letting Trewithick cover the front.

'Josh! Josh! Where are you?' shouted his mother's voice.

He gripped his sword and remembered that he was in the dark, watching for scarecrows dragging their feet along the road.

A movement caught the corner of his eye. He spun but there was nothing, no one there.

He was alone in the dark. Trewithick had been moving too fast for him to keep up going backwards.

'Mr. Trewithick,' he called turning this way and that to find his teacher. Around him creatures shuffled towards him from all direction.

Except towards the Village Green. He raised his sword to cut a way, then he stopped. Trewithick couldn't have moved that fast, carrying the hefty lass.

He's right here, thought Josh. *I could see him if I knew how look in the right way.*

'Mr. Trewithick,' he said, trying to remain calm. 'I can't see you.'

For a long moment there was no response. Panic built twisting Josh's stomach.

Then, *'He lets us see clearly in the darkness,'* Trewithick said. 'Can you see me now, Josh?'

Josh turned, panting with fear that there would be nothing.

Trewithick stood three feet from his side.

He nodded, unable to express his relief at seeing his teacher.

'They seem to be targeting you as weakest,' Trewithick said. 'I'm impressed, son. Most trainees would have run off to look for me. How about we just jog to the van. Now.'

The borrowed raincoat flapped open. To busy to retie it, Josh forced his pace to stay at Trewithick's side even though he wanted to race to the van.

At the edge of the village, more scarecrows rushed out of the hedgerow.

Trewithick dumped the girl to her feet and slashed at the nearest.

With glazed eyes, she sank into a crouch. Josh set his back to her and cut at the nearest arm.

It fell to the ground but the glove-hand continued crawling. He stomped on it, holding it in place while he slashed at the rest of the creature, finally cutting it apart.

'Josh, grab the girl and run for the van.' Backing slightly, Trewithick stuffed the keys into his free hand then returned to slash at the next lump of animated hay.

Josh dropped the keys into a pocket. 'I'll lock her in and come back.'

'No! Stay with her. Don't sleep! There's a flask of coffee in the front. And don't, under any circumstance, open the van until dawn.'

'What about you, sir?'

'I'll be fine without two people to protect,' shouted Trewithick. 'I've got to restore balance here. Go!'

Josh grabbed the girl's hand and tugged her to her feet. It felt like he was dragging a sack of coal but she staggered after him.

He slashed at the scarecrow in the way and pulled her along the road.

Squinting through the rain, Josh saw the way to the van was clear. He upped his pace, pulling hard on his burden.

Six scarecrows loomed out of the night.

Josh dropped her wrist and she sagged to the road.

Lifting the sword, he felt the night energies coalescing in the blade. They sang in his head and heart, until it felt as if something would explode.

'Go! Away!' he shouted and swung the sword.

It felt like an explosion in his stomach. Darkness flared from the sword, blocking out the bright flashes of lightning. Then a star ignited in his head, and the light flowed out as he swung the blade. Even the scarecrows untouched by the sword crumbled. The straw unraveled slowly, drifting in a vast void. He grinned inanely as the wind caught the now empty clothes, snatching them high into the air.

For one brief moment he had been the Universe.

Now he was just Josh. Pain stabbed through his knees and his neck could barely hold up a head too heavy for his sapped strength.

For the first few steps he used the sword as a walking stick as he staggered towards the van. Behind him he felt fires flare, as Trewithick too called on the strength they taught at college.

Pulling out the keys, Josh hoped that the girl would follow. It reassured him to hear her feet pounding the road behind him. Josh tugged open the rear doors and stuffed the girl inside. Josh considered ignoring the command to stay in here, but he wasn't sure that his legs would carry him back up the road.

He took a last glance over his shoulder and saw Trewithick hacking at straw creatures burning so fiercely that the wind only whipped the flames into greater fury. Not even the pelting rain could douse them.

Josh climbed in and slammed the door.

He jabbed at the door lock then paused to catch his breath. By touch he found Trewithick's lantern torch and turned it on. Above his head rain drummed impatient fingers on the roof.

He turned to the girl. She pushed her hair out of her face and Josh got a shock. The woman was older than he was, probably in her mid-twenties.

It was Samantha.

'What the hell do you think you were playing at?' he growled.

'I wanted to see what all the fuss was about,' she said. 'We may have just moved here, but no one tells *me* that women don't go somewhere.'

'Sometimes rituals are made for a reason,' Josh said. He pointed at the back door. 'You know those things out there? They wanted to rape you.'

She turned white. 'Nonsense. It's all just mass hysteria.'

Josh rolled his eyes. Then he sat with his back against one wall of the van and his feet on the other, blocking the way out. He laid his sword across his knee. 'Settle in, we've got all night.'

He eased out of the raincoat that Trewithick had loaned him, so that he wouldn't drip on the mattress Trewithick kept in the back of the van for when he did an overnighter. He tried to fling it to one side, but in the rush to get inside the belt had caught in the door as it shut. He reached across to the latch, then remembered Trewithick's admonishment not to open the van under any circumstances. The belt would have to trail out in the night.

He hoped Trewithick was fine. He had looked hard-pressed

A bang sounded on the door: a frantic pounding.

'Josh! Josh! Open the door! Quick!'

Josh leaned forwards to the latch. Then hesitated. Fighting every instinct to help his master he drew his hand away from the door.

'Go on open it!' said the woman. 'He's in real trouble.'

'Josh! Help!'

Josh leaned back against the wall. He clenched his hands around the sword hilt. He stared at the other wall where Trewithick had hung a wolf spear and a shotgun.

'Open it!'

He shook his head and wouldn't look at her.

'Josh! Josh!' The cry was strangled this time. He could imagine the scarecrows ripping Trewithick apart with their gloved hands.

'Move aside, boy.' She pushed at him, trying to reach the latch.

'Josh! Samantha! Help!'

Josh pushed back. 'How does he know your name? It was too dark to see who you were.'

The woman opened her mouth to speak then shut it. She leaned against the back of the front seats, looking anywhere but at him.

He lifted his knees and rested his chin on the sword's pommel.

'Thanks for coming to my rescue,' said Samantha.

Josh shrugged. 'Actually that's our job. To help people in need. Sounds a bit knight errant-y, I know.'

'How do you get into this line of work?'

Josh shrugged again. 'It's a sort of vocation, you... well, it's a calling.'

'Like a monk?'

'What, Trewithick?' Josh sniggered. 'From what I've heard, there's not much that's monk-like about any of us. I'd never join that sort of thing, though my Mum thinks I've gone mad studying theology.'

She shivered. Both he and Trewithick wore raincoats--she was soaked in the skirt and light cotton shirt worn for the dance earlier. He shifted slightly.

'If you move over here you can wear the raincoat. It's caught in the door, but you'd be warmer with it on.'

She edged around him and wrapped the coat around her shoulders. She shivered again.

'Can you hold me?' she whispered.

Josh rolled his eyes. 'I'm supposed to be guarding you. I can't do that with you tucked under my shoulder.'

'They can't get in here or they wouldn't be trying to lure us out by trickery.'

Josh sighed. 'For a bit then.'

She shuffled along mattress and Josh wrapped an arm around her. He kept one hand on the sword. Samantha snuggled into his side.

After a while of silence, her breathing deepened into sleep. Josh shook her slightly.

'We're not supposed to sleep.'

She didn't wake.

It was probably just him who had to stay awake. He had to remain on guard. Through the front windscreen, misted by their breath, he could see shapes drifting about. They bumped against the van, sometimes they would call out in voices he knew.

Josh tightened his hand on the sword; it felt right in his hand. Even in this shielded van, the energies surged up the blade, giving him a delicious feeling, like pins and needles in his heart.

A gust of wind rocked the van. He sat up sharply. He yawned, blinking fiercely to keep awake.

Coffee. He needed the coffee in the flask on the front seat. He shifted to reach for it, but Samantha's arms tightened around him. He moved, dragging her with him.

Her eyes blinked open. She smiled sleepily at him. Outside the shuffling had gone quiet.

'You're really nice, Josh.' She lifted her face as an invitation.

He leaned forwards for the coffee. Samantha misread the move. Gently, her warm lips searched out his. He tightened his arm around her shoulder pulling her closer; her lips were soft.

Her kiss felt like dust.

His hand convulsed around the sword hilt. Kissing seemed so insignificant, compared to the feeling of ecstasy that had happened when he had ordered the scarecrows to dissolve.

With his free hand between them he tried to push her back.

She reached up with her left hand to pull his head to her. A glint of gold on the third finger panicked Josh. He pushed harder.

The creatures outside had called up his Mum's voice earlier, now it was Josh's turn to recall her rules.

'You're a good boy Josh,' said Mum. 'You don't mess with married women.'

'Stop it, Samantha,' he said.

She grabbed at him with both arms around his neck to drag him onto the mattress. He batted her arms away and broke the hold. He ducked out of immediate reach.

While her eyes were open her face was blank as she reached for him again, her lips pursed in an obscene parody of passion.

'Give over,' he said. Then louder. 'Hey stop!'

He batted at her groping hands again. She shuffled over the van towards him, the way the missing limbs from the scarecrows had moved.

Like she was sleepwalking.

Oh God! They got into her head, Josh thought. He shook her shoulder. 'Wake up! Samantha! Wake up!'

She smiled sleepily and grabbed the hand on her shoulder.

Josh tried to pull his hand away, but the grip she had on him was powerful.

Dragging the sword with him, he shuffled away from her towards the front of the van. He was leaving the door unguarded, but she was more intent on coming after him than opening the van.

It puzzled him how the scarecrows were affecting Samantha. Okay, so he'd only been at the college for a month and bit but still he knew that even without all the wards, the van should be safe--the rubber tires isolated it from ground. Was it just because she was asleep?

He had to wake her. But he remembered that you weren't supposed to waken sleepwalkers.

She made another lunge for his lips with her mouth.

The sword clanged to the floor as he grabbed her by both shoulders and shook hard. 'Wake up!' he shouted.

The glazed expression slipped for a second then the look of bovine cunning dropped back over her face.

He shook her harder. She wrapped her arms around his neck and began to smooch. This time the kisses were warm and welcome. He let his hands slide from her shoulder. One dropped to her waist, the other groped her breast. Kneading the plump handful, he shifted his weight to pull her closer. His knee brushed against the glacial warmth of the sword.

Her breath smelled like musty old straw.

He pushed her away in disgust. Starfire burned up his leg and cleared his mind. In utter panic, he slapped her face and slithered out of her hold. She pulled away, blinking hard.

He paused, hoping that he'd broken the control of the scarecrows, but with a puzzled frown on her face she dived after him. He had hesitated too long; he expected the impact right on his chest, but she fell short. The trapped belt on the raincoat held her back.

Looking at the door, he saw it. The bright soul light of the scarecrows was gushing up the belt, following the open channel through the steel--hard wards that Trewithick had set on his van.

The belt must be touching the ground outside. He flung himself across the van and grabbed the belt in both hands. He tugged hard.

The shut door held the belt tight.

He tugged harder as Samantha crawled over the van. She caught hold of his foot and began to slide up his leg.

He yanked on the belt desperate to break the link with ground. His only fear was the belt would rip, leaving the contact.

Her hands crept up to the waistband of his jeans and her ready fingers found the button.

Desperately, he jerked on the belt of the raincoat as she started on the zip.

'Stop it!' he yelled. With a vicious backhand, he flung her across the van.

As her head banged on the ash staff of the wolf spear, she blinked.

The belt had moved with her weight pulling it.

He yanked hard on the fabric and, with a final tug, the belt slid into the van.

The wards on the van smothered the soul light.

Her face brightened into true wakefulness. 'What? What happened?'

'You tried to seduce me!' he said, through gritted teeth. Lifting the sword and pointing it at her he added, 'You stay back.'

'I wouldn't do that!' Her face flushed, indignantly. 'I was dreaming, you...'

Josh took deep breaths--he had a filthy taste of straw in his mouth. 'Mr. Trewithick said we shouldn't sleep. There's a flask of coffee on the front seat. Reach it over, I think it might be a long night.'

* * * *

When first light fell on the windscreen, Josh climbed out and stretched. Tattered remnants of scarecrows littered the ground. He heard the creaking of the van's suspension.

'Well, that's the end of the Scarecrow Festival,' said Samantha, staring around.

Trewithick sat on a wall nearby. He looked wet, but the storm had blown over. His sword cane leaned against the wall at his feet. As the van opened, he dropped his hand behind the wall, in a guilty way.

'I took plenty of notes yesterday. That storm's really ripped them up, but we can still award prizes.' He frowned at her. 'You can return to your house now, madam. No doubt there is a place for feminism, but the old traditions are not that place.'

She glared at him, but stalked away, without saying another word, to where the first risers of the morning were looking out onto the storm damage.

Josh walked over to Trewithick and smelled cigarette smoke.

'I didn't know you smoked,' he said. 'Doesn't it get in the way of this work?'

Trewithick lifted his hand from behind the wall with a wry smile. 'I'm very fit, and in year six you learn how to heal yourself--that includes self-inflicted damage.'

His hair had fallen free of the ponytail ribbon. Josh could see streaks of gray and remembered this man was over forty--the usual retirement age for this job.

'You might want to put your coat back on,' Trewithick said. 'Before her husband comes out and sees lipstick on your shirt.'

Josh looked down, startled to see a smear of pink on his chest.

'We didn't...' He could feel a flush rising in his cheeks.

Trewithick grinned.

'Sir,' Josh glanced up. 'I wasn't even interested I... The power I used...'

'First times of anything can be very intense,' Trewithick said. 'But it wears off, shortly.' He paused as if wondering whether to say more, then said, 'Any coffee left?'

'There might be a cup.' Josh retrieved the flask from the back of the van.

'I asked a lot from such a very new first year, and you didn't fail me. Thank you,' Trewithick said.

Josh poured out the dregs from the flask. 'The other apprentices warned me that your tutorials could get hairy.'

Flying Start

Dear Philip,

Karl's not the only who needs to learn how to protect himself. I was horrified to hear from your Dad that you're in hospital with burns. Why didn't you tell me?

Are you still determined to take up that place in Edinburgh reading Atmospheric Chemistry? I wish you would reconsider.

I've been thinking, I can't stay this ignorant. After this last couple of years I feel like I've got victim *tattooed on my forehead. So I decided to go and take a look at the coven the others...*

Where was that buzzing coming from?

Penny frowned and looked around the lobby of the Natural Fertility Center. The receptionist was on the phone, talking with that false cheeriness that is required for the job. The noise didn't seem to be coming from the computer--it was turned off.

Electricity could sometimes hum. Penny looked up to see if the lights were on. Her jaw dropped and she flushed. It was a good job the lights weren't on, she was sure she didn't want to look at the ceiling art too closely.

Penny shook her head sharply. That buzzing was getting really irritating. She folded her copy of the Radio Times into her handbag, at the page she had reached in planning next week's viewing--being the in the sixth form was great, she had a television in her bedroom--then she tried to work out if the noise was tinnitus or external.

It had started as a low hum, just as she had entered through the impressive gateway. The hum had been easy to ignore as she had stared at the couples walking together over the immaculate lawn or sitting on ornate benches under perfectly manicured trees.

And now the hum had turned into a low buzzing.

A door marked *staff only* opened behind the reception desk and Chloë strode out.

'Bracken is delighted that you finally agreed to come and have a look around,' Chloë said.

Penny hid her reservations behind a friendly smile. She glanced at the white marble steps, which glowed with purity in the late afternoon sun. Her last chance to get away. Chloë tucked Penny's hand into her elbow and Penny resigned herself to actually going through with looking around.

After all, no one could expect her to commit herself without serious thought.

It's a nice looking place. Though I think they hired the same designer as your Dad. All a bit too rock star-y for me. The front door was gilded! And the ceiling even had the same sort of paintings as the hall at home. Well, I suppose it is a fertility clinic, but you could have stood me on a rock and called me a lighthouse, with my face burning like that.

The clients all looked blissfully happy. I bet they put something in that chemical-free well water that they advertise as being so good for the body.

Behind the *staff only* door the décor was more functional. Where the lobby had Milton Carpets and Laura Ashley wallpaper, behind the door the floor was covered in linoleum and the walls would look better with the paint refreshed.

'Bracken's really taught us a lot,' Chloë said.

'I thought that book of yours wouldn't have it down properly,' Penny said. She looked around. 'Can you hear anything?'

Chloë glanced at her. 'What sort of thing?'

'A buzzing sort of noise.'

Chloë shook her head. 'Are you sure your ears aren't clogged from swimming yesterday?'

'That's probably it,' Penny said. 'So what do you do here?'

'We study,' Chloë said. 'Actually, Bracken has us reading a lot of books.'

Penny shrugged. She hoiked her handbag strap further up on her shoulder. At the end of the maze of corridors, Chloë tapped on door labeled *Manager*.

'Come in.'

Chloë opened the door. 'I've brought Penny.'

'Oh, come in dear, and bring your friend.'

Chloë held the door. 'Penny this is Bracken.'

Penny noted that the name on the door was Edith Cubb.

Chloë did this weird little genuflection as she entered.

Penny raised an eyebrow, but kept a smile on her face, as a woman in a business suit a size too small for her matronly figure emerged from behind a desk.

Her hair was dyed black and deliberately worked into rats-tails. From behind the desk a black cat jumped onto the desk. It offered Penny the standard cat-ly disapproving look.

Bracken walked forward holding out her hand. 'Penny dear, lovely to meet you at last.'

Penny took the offered grip--it was cool and firm. 'I'm pleased to meet you. Chloë and the others in our study group talk about you all the time.'

The woman smiled, but her gaze held Penny's. 'Since you are here to look around, I can assume that it is mostly favorable.'

'Of course it is, Bracken,' Chloë gushed. 'We could never find a bad thing to say about this coven.'

Bracken's smile remained plastered on, but her eyes flicked towards Chloë with a slight roll.

She returned to looking at Penny. 'Chloë tells me your family were involved in the Cræft. Have you studied?'

'A little,' Penny said. 'Enough to be able to bail the girls out when they messed up the garden spell. I know a lot about how love spells go wrong.'

'And you're an orphan now? That's so sad.'

You're going to get a great deal out of pleasure out of 'I told you so' when I see you in the summer hols. It's just that I don't feel comfortable telling the girls that I live with my Mum's ex-husband. If I told them I was living with your lot, then I'd have to tell them why mum's in prison. It's not something I'm proud of.

'Sort of,' Penny said. She looked out the window. Beyond the lawn she could see a plantation of trees. 'Nice place you've got here. Tell me what do you do?'

Bracken stopped her probing. 'We help couples who have difficulty conceiving, of course. The relaxed atmosphere and meditation often works without intervention.'

'But sometimes you have to intervene?' Penny turned back to Bracken.

'Sometime we request our nature spirit to intervene.' Bracken paused. 'We like new people to meet with our spirit--that's the easiest way to discover whether a person fits in here.'

'But we haven't--' Chloë started but was frowned down by Bracken.

'Of course *you* haven't dear, but Penny admitted to having some training outside of our coven. When you are trained you will meet the spirit to see if you can continue here. I need for you to call everyone together for the evening gathering at the Temple.'

Chloë looked hurt as she backed out of the office.

Penny hitched the handbag strap up onto her shoulder again. 'So when are you planning on next summoning your nature spirit.'

And I can be busy on that evening, thought Penny.

'We don't need a special night to summon our spirit,' said Bracken. 'Is that what you are used to? No, I'll take you to the sanctum. It stays there most of the time.'

'I thought a night's vigil with the spirit came later in the program,'

Penny said.

'You won't be doing that tonight,' said Bracken. 'I just want you to meet our spirit.'

'Okay then,' Penny said, regretting her words a moment later.

Bracken's smile broadened. 'If you'll follow me. I'll show you around the center first--it's on our way.'

I have to admit it was just like I was expecting--which is why I put off visiting for so long. I'm not really into meditation and special diets. And they use too much incense...

Penny sneezed as Bracken opened another door into the public areas of the center. She pushed aside the *Radio Times* in her handbag to find her packet of tissues while trying to hold onto another sneeze.

Blowing her nose, Penny tried to look apologetic. Bracken kept her practiced smile in place.

'We find that the relaxed atmosphere in this clinic helps everyone-- including the staff. We have a very low staff turnover. The sauna and spa are around here.'

Bracken led Penny along a mosaic-tiled corridor. The mosaic pattern was standard fish and mermaids pattern that one might expect for a water therapy area, all blue and aqua.

The air was warm and moist, uncomfortable for someone fully dressed. But most of the blissed-out clientele were in robes with NFC embroidered on the left breast.

Penny wafted a hand in front of her face as she tried to breathe very shallowly--the sticky air was full of scents and spices.

'As you can see we offer a full spa facility. Follow me.'

Thankfully Bracken led Penny into cooler air.

She waved at a grand staircase. 'The meditation chambers are above the spa, but walking in the garden is also good relaxation for our clients.'

Bracken shook her head as she walked into a living room. She touched her ear and frowned slightly.

Did she hear the buzzing too? It was subliminal to the whole building.

Then the smile was back on Bracken's face as she opened a French window and stepped out onto a patio. Roses, growing in stone urns, blanketed the still, evening air with their fragrance. Penny tried not to be too obvious as she shied away from the vast pots of thorns.

'The temple is at the bottom of the garden,' said Bracken. She led the way down the cleanest stone steps Penny had ever seen: no algae or lichen on these treads. No paths marred the plush lawn--it was like walking on carpet. Bracken took Penny through a cool thicket of Rhododendrons and they were at the compost heaps.

Penny glanced at Bracken, but the older woman continued towards the heaps. Through the thicket she could hear more people converging on this spot. Penny raised an eyebrow--she had expected a more inviting location for their fertility temple.

A marble-walled Grecian folly with a domed roof rose from behind the compost, but the white walls were flecked with slime from where the gardeners had missed the heaps with their rubbish.

'Here, we are dear,' said Bracken.

Penny picked her way around the compost heaps. It seemed an odd place to put your temple--though when she thought about it, a fertility temple near a compost heap was sort of logical, if off-putting.

The staff emerged from the thicket and formed into a circle around the compost heaps. Penny could see Chloë among them; she glowered at Penny.

Penny hitched her handbag back up her shoulder. 'Okay then. Aren't you coming in too?' she added as she watched Bracken holding open the door for her. The buzzing was much louder here.

'Our spirit would get confused if someone it already knew came in when trying to get to know a stranger.'

With a backward glance to where she thought the main park entrance was located, Penny strode inside.

She had expected cool, but it was warm and clammy in here, as if some of the heat from the saunas had been diverted here. Fertility temple, warm--again it made a sort of sense.

They should at least have cleared away the offerings, thought Penny as she looked around in the dim light from the still partly open door. Plates of food looked like they had been in place on the stone slab altar for days. *Well, it's not as if there are supplicants here tonight I suppose.*

Where the columns stood on the outside, there were rough stone uprights and lintels. Opposite the door lay an old stone slab covered in lichen, even though it was inside. Near each plate was an incense stick-- Penny was grateful for that. She could see maggots crawling in the food on the altar now.

She took shallow breaths through her mouth. She really didn't want to smell the rotting offerings, but a drift of incense caught her throat and she started coughing.

Through watering eyes she saw a figure standing behind the altar. Penny took another step forward. A strange buzzy hymn sounded through the open door.

The figure stepped out from behind the altar. Penny frowned. She had heard its footsteps on the stone floor--apparently this creature wore boots.

Penny shifted her grip on her handbag. The creature stalked forwards through the smoke.

It had a fly head.

Penny stepped back towards the door. That explained the maggots then. Closer to the light coming through the door, Penny could see the creature carved on the old stone uprights.

A fly-headed man--very clearly a man, the pictures wore no clothes. But the creature in front of her was wearing a robe--and boots.

Penny squinted through the smoke. The creature lifted up an arm to embrace her. Outside the song turned into buzzy welcome.

Penny swung her handbag. It impacted on a solid man. He sprawled through the open door. The mask he was wearing skidded down the steps.

The hymn stopped mid-phrase and turned into a collective gasp.

'But it's a man in mask!' Chloë said. 'It's all trickery!'

Following the man onto the front steps of the folly, Penny saw Chloë's eyes glinting in the last of the sunlight as if holding unshed tears.

'What were you expecting, Chloë? Fairy tale magic?' Penny said.

'But I saw you... you and the Mr. Dunkley... you did...'

Penny shook her head. 'I tried to tell you, but I think you were hallucinating from smoke inhalation.'

Chloë stepped away shaking her head. 'NO! I saw...!' For a moment more she stared with wide-open eyes at the man who was pushing himself to his knees. Then she turned and ran through the gathered staff members.

Everyone stared at the man who no longer wore a mask.

Penny felt a wrench in her gut for lying, but Chloë was better off out of that world. She turned back to Bracken.

Bracken clenched her fists as she glared up at Penny.

Penny gave her bag a little swing.

Bracken unclenched her fists and walked up the steps. Her gaze bore into Penny's face.

Bracken made a flicking gesture with her hand and stalked into the temple. Penny followed, still holding her bag ready as a weapon.

'This is just what I expected,' Penny said. 'So why did you choose a fly-headed spirit for your fertility clinic--surely a bunny-headed one would be more appropriate?'

'Flies are very fecund creatures.' Bracken gestured at the plates of decaying food, maggots crawled in them. 'And there was the art work on the stone circle we found here.'

The buzzing grew louder.

Penny blinked. 'Are you telling me you've been faking worship on the site of an old temple?'

Bracken drew herself up. 'We're not faking.'

Penny darted glances around the Grecian-style temple. She started backing towards the door. 'Bracken,' she whispered. 'We need to get out of here. Now!'

Bracken smiled smugly. 'I thought you didn't believe in the fairy tale stuff.'

The stone of the altar shattered, spraying lichenous stone around the room.

Penny ducked her head, sheltering her eyes in her elbows. Squinting up, she could see a creature. It's translucent wings buzzed loudly in the clammy air. It was the size of a man, with a man's body. But this was no fairy--on top of that well-fit body was set a fly's head.

'I'm zzzick of the humanz wanting offzzpring. I wanz my own.'

'Bracken!' Penny shouted. 'We've got to get out NOW!'

Bracken stared, mouth open wide, at the creature hovering in the air.

Penny grabbed Bracken's arm and tugged her to the door.

Bracken was rooted to the spot, mouth open, staring at the impossible.

The creature waved a hand and the door slammed shut. Dropping Bracken's arm, Penny ran to the door and thumped into it with all her force.

'Let me out!' she screamed and kicked at the door.

It was firmly locked.

Penny turned around and stared at the source of the buzzing.

Penny pressed back against the door. 'You stay away from me.'

The buzzing increased into a laugh. 'You arez Mine.'

The creature began a buzzy little song, very like the hymn the people outside had been singing. It weaved from side to side, buzzing happily.

It was a horror.

Bracken watched the weaving creature and began swaying in time with the creature's movements. Her gaze was fixed on the disco-oscillation of the compound eyes.

With spider footfalls, Penny crept towards Bracken, trying not to attract the creature's hypnotizing attention.

The buzzing singsong drove everything out of her head.

Penny tried to get her thoughts in order. She needed to think. She needed an idea about how to get out of here, but every time she had a nagging in her brain, that told her an idea was on the way, the buzzing interrupted it.

Why was it always up to her to sort out other people's messes? Just for once in her life she had wanted everything to go right. Instead, there was another creature on the loose, and it was up to her lock it away again. She couldn't call for help, because she there was no back up near. She had no training to deal with these monsters, because training women was left to the covens. And when she had tried to join a coven, *this* happened. Again.

And that awful buzzing rattled her brain.

'Shut up!' she shouted, tearing her hands through her hair.

To her amazement the flyman fell silent. With vast compound eyes it looked at her. If a fly could look puzzled this one did.

Penny blinked. Okay if it took orders then... 'Now let us out!'

'Zzilly girlz. Why izzzz you not tranzzzzed?'

Bracken blinked. She looked around in a dazed way.

The creature re-started buzzing and weaving. Bracken relaxed into her tranced swaying.

Then Penny caught feel of rising power. From outside the fetid walls she could hear singing--human voices trying to mimic the buzzing of the flyman--and with that belief the creature would get stronger.

She had to do something NOW.

Clearly satisfied that Bracken was under its spell the creature turned back to Penny.

'ZzzI'll take you firzzzt,' the creature hummed. 'ZzzHonoured. You will carry my offspringzzzz.'

'I'll do nothing of the sort,' Penny said.

Reaching into her bag, she stirred the mess in a desperate attempt to find her Mace spray--with those eyes it would have to hurt.

Nothing.

The creature buzzed closer.

'You are minezzzz.'

It lunged forward, wings buzzing.

Penny grabbed the first thing--her copy of the *Radio Times*.

'Stay back or I'll... I'll swat you into the middle of next week.'

Again there was that buzzing laughter. 'Zze human conzept of time applyzzzzz not to my kindzzzz.'

It landed and reached for her. 'You will be my matez.'

Taking advantage of the lull in buzzing as it folded its wings, Penny gathered her strength and slammed the Radio Times at one of the creature's huge eyes.

'You asked for it!' she screamed.

'Noooooo!'

To her astonishment the creature dissolved. On her magazine there was a splat--like a swatted fly. Penny looked at the splat--then she looked more closely. At 3.45pm on Wednesday of next week, the children's educational programming listed the *Lifecycle of the Housefly*.

Quickly, she folded it into her handbag. That program had to have been there all along.

The door swung open.

Bracken blinked in the brighter light. 'Where is he? What happened to our God?'

Penny pointed out the door to where the man, who had been in the fly mask, stood.

'He's there.'

'No!' Bracken said. 'The real God. What do you do to him?'

'You use too much incense in here,' Penny said. 'Now *you're* hallucinating.'

Penny stalked through the door. The whole coven was gathered around the compost heaps, all blinking as if they had woken from a daze.

At the top step Penny spun around. 'And which insane person chose a *fly* as a fertility spirit?'

It turned out to be not my sort of thing, so I'll not bother going back.

Love Penny.

Dreaming at the Edge of Light

Sometimes, late at night, the Underground can be an odd place. But Joe, who worked the graveyard shift at a burger bar on Oxford Street, liked to watch people as they got off and on. It was amazing, considering how large the population of London was, that he sometimes recognized the people from other journeys. He liked to think that girl must be a pop star slumming it, and that old homeless bloke was a millionaire looking for someone to sponsor into a better life.

One night a stranger got into the same carriage as Joe. His hair was tied back in a ponytail and blond, which was odd as most adults lose their childhood fairness long before thirty and he looked closer to forty.

As the closing doors trapped the light that had poured in at the station, and the platform slowly moved away, the man moved across the swaying floor with the natural balance of a dancer.

The dark tunnel reached out and swallowed the train. Outside, as blank walls flashed past, light from the carriage briefly pushed the deep shadows into hiding.

The man looked around the quiet carriage then flung his suit jacket over the gym bag dumped on the seat next to him. Sitting down, he rubbed the eyebrow above his right eye as if he had a headache. With the comforting rattle of wheels on the track singing him a lullaby, he leaned his head against the carriage window.

Joe lost interest in the man once those sea-gray eyes had closed, aside from hoping the man wasn't a snorer. He opened his sketchbook and pulled his pencil from the chest pocket of his burger bar uniform shirt. Now he could continue with his drawing of the girl in fantasy sword-fighter get up. As she was on the carriage tonight, he wanted to get her nose right. One day he would write the greatest graphic novel ever. They'd make it into a film. He would win awards.

Holding the trophy over his head he cries, 'I'd like to thank...'

The train shuddered to a stop. The carriage lights went out. The emergency exit sign fizzled a little then the carriage was dark.

In Joe's hand the pencil snapped. Darkness muffled the noise as the two ends clattered on the worn linoleum of the carriage floor.

'Did anyone else hear a bang?' asked Joe, his voice mouse-thin from fear. 'Do you think it's a terrorist?'

'It happened last week,' said a female voice in the dark. 'We're near where they're digging the tunnel for the new line. I bet the workers have cut through a cable again.'

A torch came on. 'Is everyone all right?' asked a resonant male voice. Joe could imagine hearing that voice on a stage from the back of the hall. It had studied at the best schools.

From the position of the torchlight, Joe decided it must be the stranger.

'Yeah, fine,' said the girl. Other people muttered reassurances. 'Now we sit and wait. Wake me when the lights come on.'

The strong light turned the girl's snuggle down under her coat into a shadow play against the white walls. If his pencil had been whole it would have been the perfect image to capture for the maiden warrior asleep in the forest.

Three other people in the carriage crept towards the safety of the stranger's torch. Joe watched their shadows sneaking up behind them, trying to crowd out the light.

Joe fought the urge to join them.

A shadow swirled in the deeper dark outside the windows. He jerked his head to see, but there was nothing there. He flicked glances to the other windows hoping to catch whatever was out there, but it was just a glimmer.

Another light entered the carriage through the adjoining door to the rear of the train. The guard, followed by a posse of train passengers, walked through.

'All right folks,' he said. 'I've got a message through from the driver. He says that we can't get the train started again tonight, so we've got to walk the 300 yards to the next station. Once we're off, they can tow the train out of the way. We've got station staff coming to light the way.'

The girl groaned, but picked up her coat and bag, and joined the crocodile of people who followed the guard forward through the train.

Joe eyed the world outside window. It was dark out there, but the guard and the stranger were taking the only lights with them, out of the train.

As the stranger shrugged into his suit jacket and zipped up his gym bag preparing to join with the exodus, Joe knew he had to follow. He stuffed his sketchbook into his pocket. The dark already reached into the carriage as the guard opened the door into the next coach and led his little parade through.

The stranger waved Joe on and took the rear position without being asked. He had the torch trained at the floor. As they stepped over the chasm into the next carriage, Joe saw the rails glinting.

Come to me, the night whispered through the gap.

He hurried after the gang through the next carriage and over the next rift into the dark. This was the last coach.

The driver stood at the final door, helping passengers down to the waiting hands below.

A trickle of cold sweat ran down Joe's back. Out there it was dark. Firefly lights bobbed as the station staff led stranded passengers along the rails, and up ahead lights shined like the gates of heaven, where it opened into the next station.

It's not like 300 yards is a long distance, thought Joe. That was less than 300 meters. He could swim that distance easily--in a brightly-lit swimming pool.

Come to me, Joe, whispered the dark.

The guard shuffled past them and took his torch back along the train. 'I've just got to check one more time that there's no one left on the train. T'other week we had had someone so scared of the dark she hid under a seat. Took three of us to carry her out.'

No friendly light awaited them on the track.

'Wait here a moment,' said the driver. 'We've got to wait for one of the station staff to come back to get you. We don't want you tripping up in the dark.'

'I've got my torch,' said the stranger. 'I've got an appointment. I can still make it if I get a taxi.'

'Well,' said the driver. 'As long as you know I warned you that it's not safe out there.'

'You've turned off the electric rail, surely?'

'Well, of course, but you could still trip,' said the driver. 'Anyway, follow the rail straight to the station. You won't go wrong that way. There's some old tunnels here that got closed off after the war, but the construction crew are sounding them out for building the new line.'

The stranger laid the torch on the floor and dropped to the ground outside. Shouldering his gym bag, he picked up the torch and ran it over Joe.

He was taking away the light.

'Are you coming too, Joe?' asked the stranger.

Licking his lips, Joe nodded. 'I've got to get to work.'

'That's the boy.'

Joe jumped down and huddled into the little world-globe of light. *How did he know my name?*

But it was too late to turn back. All around them the darkness pressed in, an airless void that would take them the moment all the air was used up in the bright space capsule in which they traveled.

40

Joe, come to me, whispered the night.

'Help me,' shouted a weak voice. 'I'm trapped.'

It sounded like a woman's voice, but that must be wrong. Joe knew there weren't that many female construction workers.

'Help me,' shouted the voice again. This time it was deeper. Ah! That explained it. The first time the voice had been girly from fear. Joe looked round in the dark. The voice was stronger down that side tunnel.

'It must be coming from down here,' he said. 'Come on.'

The stranger looked at him oddly. 'I beg your pardon?'

'The trapped construction worker,' said Joe. He ran off into the dark.

'Joe, stop!'

The light faded quickly into a twilight that kept up with him.

'Find me, please,' said the voice. It was quieter now.

'I'm coming, just hold on,' shouted Joe. 'I'll get you out.'

He came out onto the station concourse. People hailed him a hero who had saved the life of this man when his co-workers hadn't even noticed he was missing. The lights of the newspaper cameras flashed. Joe blushed modestly.

'When I heard him calling in the dark, I just had to go.'

'Even though you're afraid of the dark?' asked a reporter.

Joe shrugged. 'Perhaps I have overcome it now. By facing it down for another person, maybe I can get a proper job in the daytime now.'

The girl he had been drawing in the carriage leaned against him. 'You're so brave,' she whispered in his ear. Her breath was warm on his neck.

'I'm here, Joe,' whispered the voice in the dark. 'Rescue me, and all that could be yours. I can give you anything you want.'

Joe cradled the man in his arms and staggered back through the dark tunnels. The man had gone silent. Ahead of him he could see a light.

'Joe!'

Joe thought the shout came from the stranger from the train. For moment he was grateful.

'He'll steal your glory,' said the voice. 'Hide away!'

Joe could see it. *'Here Joe, let me carry him for you,' said the stranger. Joe relinquished his burden and trailed into the station behind the golden stranger. The girl, he had been drawing in carriage, now leaned into the stranger. Her breath warmed his neck instead.*

Joe cuddled the man against his chest. The voice was warm in his ear.

'Joe!' came the shout again, then oddly, 'All mine enemies whisper together against me.'

And Joe realized that he was alone in the dark, with the voices. He cradled something cold and smooth in his arms. His flesh crawled where it touched his bare arm. It clanged on an old rail as he dropped it.

Blindly, he swung about trying to find the way back. He walked forward, holding out his arms like a zombie. Two paces then his hands struck the wall. He felt the cool tiles on his fingertips. Which way should he go to get out of here?

'This way, Joe,' whispered the voice in the dark, just behind him. 'You can hide this way.'

He felt a sort of tug, leading off to his right.

'I can give you all your dreams.'

'STOP!' he shouted. 'Go away!' He slid down the tiled wall and curled like a shadow around a candle.

'JOE! Where are you? Call again!'

The dark void sucked the air from him. He gasped for air like a fish in a fetid pond.

'I can save you.'

Colors, sparks in his vision. Are those the stars?

Joe.'

Ten seconds, that was how long you could survive in space. The cold was already freezing the water in his cells. How long before they ruptured?

'Joe, worship me, love me, feed me, save me, Joe.'

'Stop calling me,' he whimpered.

'There's no one calling, Joe,' said a warm human voice.

Joe looked up. The light was back, delineating the shadows. Air rushed back. He could breathe.

'There is,' he gasped. 'Why can't you hear him?'

'I suspect that's because I'm warded against the voices at the edge of night. Here, try this.'

The stranger loosened his tie and opened his top button. The light glinted off a chain underneath. He didn't seem the sort to wear man-bling. He lifted it over his head and dumped the silver crucifix around Joe's neck.

The voices stopped short. The darkness faded into twilight as the strong torchlight reflected off white tile walls.

Joe stood up and looked around in amazement. 'But I heard him. Where has he gone?'

'Gone? Nowhere, it's still here. Do you want to see it in its true form, rather than the vision it has planted in your head.'

'What are you talking about? There's a worker trapped down here. I was carrying him, then...' Joe looked around blankly.

'I'll show you,' said the stranger. He crouched and opened his gym bag. 'Now what have I in here to help... Oh yes, that will do.'

Leaving his torch on the ground, he planted his feet among the rotting sleepers and the shifting ballast. He twisted the lid on a tin and shook a white powder into the air.

'Show me mine enemies.'

Instead of drifting aimlessly in the torchlight, the powder surged and twisted outlining a huge face hanging in the air. The mouth of the creature opened in a scream, but Joe heard nothing.

'What is that?' he whispered.

The stranger shrugged. 'Athlete's foot powder--no doubt they're more used to the smoke of rare incense to summon their visage, but beggars can't be choosers.'

'No!' said Joe. He pointed at the air. 'What is that... that thing?'

'That?' he said, crouching to return the tin of powder to his bag. 'It's a lar, I think.'

'A what?'

'A Roman household god.'

Joe's mouth dropped open. 'That's a god? Can it really give what it promised?'

The face adopted a kindly aspect. It smiled at Joe. Tentatively, he reached out a hand. The stranger grabbed his wrist.

'Now would be a good time to remember that the gods of one religion are the demons of the next,' said the stranger. 'Yes it can give you gifts, but what will it want in exchange from you?'

The thing snarled. Joe ducked behind the stranger.

The stranger lifted his arms. In the pale light of the torch he seemed to glow like a halo. 'Sit in the darkness being fast bound in misery and iron,' he said.

The tiles echoed his voice back to them.

A wind blew along the tunnel. It sucked the thing backwards. It grew arms and reached out, appealing to Joe, who could no longer hear its pleas.

He turned his face away and screwed his eyes shut.

Then the wind tried to pull Joe. He groped for the stranger, who wrapped a hand around Joe's wrist.

Then the wind was gone. Joe opened his eyes as the powder that had framed the creature drifted gently down, settling onto the rails and gravel like frost.

'Hmm,' said the stranger, lowering his arms. His saint-light faded. 'I wonder why someone was so frightened by that creature that they buried it in the ground. Earth would normally kill a creature of the air, it must be pretty strong to have survived that.'

43

'Are they everywhere?' said Joe, staring into the dark. 'I hear a lot of voices, that's why I work at night, so I'm awake when they try to sneak up on me.'

The stranger turned, almost as if he had forgotten Joe was there. 'Yes, creatures like that cover the air and earth, the rivers and fire. They are most often found in the dark.'

'So I'm not going mad.' Joe sighed and straightened his back. Touching the crucifix he asked, 'Can you give me something like this?'

'You can have that one,' said the man. He picked up the torch and started looking in the dark. 'But I saw your drawings. You are an artist, a dreamer, a magnet for their sort. Think on it. If you can't hear them, how can you run away?'

'How can you stand the voices without this?' Joe touched the crucifix.

'I can block them out of my mind. Like most people, I developed defenses so that, unless I'm listening, like now, I can't hear them. And they know better than to attack someone like me.'

The light picked out a carved white stone about the size of a brick. It lay where Joe had dropped it, next to the rails. The man walked over to it.

'We'll need to move this to somewhere safe.'

Joe walked over to look. It had a picture of that face carved onto it.

'It isn't heavy, I'd offer to carry it, but...'

'No, I meant my people,' said the man.

'Who are you?'

'Me? I'm Trewithick.'

'No! I think I meant, *what* are you?'

Trewithick laughed. 'I lecture in classics and theology at the University, so I know all about lares.'

'You're more than that.'

'Yes,' Trewithick said. 'But that's all you're going to know.'

'Why don't we all know about those things?'

'Ignorance is a darkness that people hide in. The wise hide in the light. Come out of the dark, Joe.'

'And how did you know my name?' asked Joe. 'Is it some mystical ability?'

The torch played over his chest and a white plastic placard.

'Your name is pinned on your shirt,' Trewithick said.

* * * *

Joe travels to work at the burger bar on Oxford Street by bus now. He has a new set of people to watch under streetlights that paint lurid patterns against the bright stars. He sketches the passengers who travel with him, through streets that never, never get dark.

Oh, and one day he's going to write the greatest graphic novel ever.

Household Gods

'That bloody machine needs an exorcist.'

Mike peered over the top of his paper, as if he had heard his name spoken. Under the fluorescent strip lights, two women glared at one of the older washing machines.

The younger woman, with her hair drawn into a ponytail on top of her head, held up a shirt. Half the sleeve was ripped off. Her name, according to the embroidery on the chest pocket of her blue polyester housecoat, was Colleen.

Bernice, an older woman with short hair, spoke next. 'It doesn't like that cheap washing powder they make us use. If it's treated right, that machine washes best of the lot.'

The women picked through the rest of the laundry pulled from the troublesome machine.

'It's going to be the scrap heap for you this time,' said Bernice. She patted the machine on the top. 'Sorry, there's nothing I can do for you.'

Through the burglar grille bolted over the window, Mike saw that the streetlights had come on. He leaned back on the window and sipped at his bottle of water, glaring at his own washing. The machine indicated it was only halfway through the program. Checking his watch he discovered he'd been sitting in the Wishing Well Wash 'O' Rama for nearly an hour now. Even with his waxed cotton jacket folded as a cushion, the seats in this place were hard. Essentially, they were windowsills.

The women took the mutilated laundry into a back room and shut the door on their gripes.

The letters page in the local paper was full of diatribes on the youth of today. To pass the time, Mike started writing a letter to the editor in his head.

Dear Sir,

>*Having just emerged from the 'youth of today' I can tell you there is nothing wrong with the youth of today that couldn't be solved by the adults of today learning to be less hide bound,*
>*Sincerely, Michael Rider*

Outside in the street, a lorry roared past. The troublesome machine rattled.

Mike stared at the washing machine suspiciously. He didn't expect to find anything, but it was something to do. He shut his eyes and whispered, 'Speak sometimes in visions to Thy saints.'

He saw, *Humans pouring their filth into a stream.* He saw, *the stream buried, hiding the filth from its creators.*

Oh No! he thought, *not sewers again*

He saw, *the construction of the temple to cleanliness.*

And Mike knew he saw through the eyes of another creature. Opening his eyes, he sighed. Even doing his laundry he could never escape from them.

I suppose, he thought, *that the creature got trapped in here and is taking revenge by ripping up the laundry.*

He pulled out a ponytail band from his jeans' pocket and tied his shoulder-length hair away from his face in work mode. Mr. Dunkley preached readiness at all times and Mike had listened--this once. Standing up and stretching, he folded his paper into his duffel bag and rummaged through for his silver bowl. He also had his bottle of mountain spring water, only half drunk. However, after a further rummage, he knocked on the staff-only door.

He grimaced at image of a cartoon fairy hovering over a wishing well, looking like a bizarre dragonfly.

The door split like a stable door. Bernice popped her head out the top half. 'Help you?'

'I was wondering if you might have any starch?' Mike asked.

Her eyebrows hit her hairline. 'What d'you want with starch?'

'Well, I do like nicely ironed shirts for work, but in this case, I think that I can help with fixing that washing machine.'

Colleen joined her colleague at the door. 'Y'wanna gum up our machine wi' starch? What's wrong wi' the spray stuff?'

Mike used his best smile. 'My mother still does it the old way. But if you're going to scrap the machine anyway, can it hurt?'

'I gotta watch this,' Colleen said.

'Unblocking a washing machine is hardly a spectator sport,' Mike said.

'S'our machine yer messing wi'.'

Mike's smile turned malicious. 'Fine.'

Opening the bottom half of the door, both women joined him in the public laundry room. With an odd look, Bernice handed him a paper packet; Colleen folded her arms and smirked.

Mike accepted the starch and mixed it up with spring water into a thin sludge in his silver bowl. He poured the mixture into the soap dispenser and turned the machine on. He stood back and gestured the women to do likewise.

Within seconds water poured out of the bottom of the machine.

'Yer wrecked it,' Colleen said. 'Told yer so.'

Mike ignored the women. 'Take thy true form.' His voice echoed in the small launderette.

The water filled an ever-expanding puddle around the machine. Bits of gummy starch mixture floated on the surface.

He scraped his thumb along the edge of the packet of starch to form a sharp pouring edge, then bent down, drawing a circle on the floor with starch powder. With his index finger, he tapped three times on the floor in front of the puddle.

'*The springs of water were seen,*' he said, in that same echoey voice.

The water gushed upward, deliberately splashing Mike on his only clean pair of jeans. Starch dust flew about and set him coughing. He stood back and glanced at the women as Bernice's mouth dropped open.

Colleen shrank away from the water. 'He musta put soda bicarb in the water. It fizzes li'...' She broke off as the water formed a pattern, which then became the image of the silly little fairy logo, standing about four feet tall.

'How dare you attack me in my own temple?' shrieked the little fairy. The starch paste dripped off her purple hair and gauzy wings onto her pink tutu.

'Your temple?' Mike folded his arms and stared down at her. She returned the glare.

'I do nothing wrong,' she said. 'Even nature-haters, like you, offer alms and supplicate me for your clothes to have their filth removed. And then you pour disgusting tasteless goo into my home.'

'Yet you tear up the clothes, after the alms have been offered and supplication made?'

'I was merely informing my priestesses that the new unguents they use are not to my taste,' said the fairy. 'If they wish proper cleanliness then they must return to the old flavor or try others until they find another I like.'

'Told you so,' crowed Bernice. She turned to Colleen. 'Didn't I tell you the machine didn't like the new powder?'

The fairy turned to the woman and nodded regally. 'You, my high priestess, are most in tune with me and read my rebuke correctly.'

'It's...' The younger woman jabbed her finger at the little figure. 'It's... it's a fairy. It's a real, bloody fairy.'

Mike grinned at Colleen. 'I told you I knew how to fix the problem.' He turned back to the enraged fairy. 'I thank you that you came at my call to explain your...'

The fairy shook off the paste, like a dog. It spattered onto an invisible wall created by the ring of starch and hung in the air. She faced Colleen. 'Does this image displease you, my priestess? It is the icon you paint on the temple walls.' She pointed at the cartoon fairy. 'I thought this representation was fair to you.'

'A priestess, heh?' said Colleen. She patted her hair. 'Like them vestal virgins I saw in the telly program?'

The fairy nodded. 'But I don't insist on virginity. One has to change priestesses so often if one does.'

The outer door of the launderette was batted open with a foot. A youth shuffled in carrying a tote bag.

Hastily, Mike wreathed shadows about himself and the fairy.

The youth looked around and saw the two women, who were frowning and trying to see where Mike and the fairy had vanished.

Colleen turned to the new customer, still casting sideways glances into the shadows. ''Cha need?'

'Y'do a service wash?' He dumped his bag at his feet.

'It's pay up front. A tenner for wash, if it all goes in one wash, plus a fiver extra for dry.'

The youth patted his pockets. 'Loan me a tenner for the wash?'

'Get away,' said Colleen. 'Come back when you got cash.'

In his shadow, Mike ignored the negotiations. 'Were there any other accommodations that you wish to discuss with your priestesses?'

'I thank you for your courtesy but no,' said the fairy. 'I will return to my place of residence. I find it pleasant to be needed and worshipped again.'

Mike lifted his hand to begin the banishment.

'Hold yer horses,' said the youth. 'I got summat here.'

Colleen turned back to him. 'A tenner?'

'Nah!' He grabbed Colleen. He had a knife at her throat. 'I gotta knife. I gonna cut yer if y'don't give me cash.'

Colleen swore at him.

'The cash is in the back room,' said Bernice. She scuttled towards the split door. She leaned inside.

Mike stepped out of the shadows. 'Stop right there!'

The youth jumped. Colleen added extra swear words to Mike's vocabulary as a line of red appeared across her throat.

''Cha gonna do? Be a hero?'

'Not me,' Mike said. He swept a foot over the circle of starch.

The paste caught by the ring splattered on the floor. He jumped back as a tidal wave of slime, starch paste and pondweed surged over the worn linoleum.

'Wha' in 'ell's name is that?' the youth shouted. The knife dropped to the floor as he sprinted for the door. Ameba-like, the slime-wave engulfed the youth's feet and rapidly slid up his legs to wrap his shoulders in a cold embrace.

'Aaaarrrggghhhh!' He tried to pull away, but the harder he wriggled the tighter the slime contracted about his arms and legs. He twisted and squirmed to keep his mouth and nose free.

Mike sighed and opened his mouth, but he was interrupted.

'No eating people,' said Bernice. She tapped the slime monster at shoulder height. 'It's really not nice, and you're making the floor all dirty.'

Slowly, so slowly, the slimy wave eased back away from the youth.

Once free he collapsed on the floor and shuffled back while he goggled the slime monster.

The slime crystallized into fairy. She sniffed at the youth and pulled a face.

'He was too dirty to eat anyway,' said the fairy. 'But no one attacks my priestesses.'

'Scare him by all means,' said the older woman. 'He doesn't look like he's going to do any more knife work.'

The four-foot fairy leaned over the cowering youth. 'Swear you will not attack my priestesses again!' She stamped a foot in some residual slime as he gibbered. 'Swear it!'

'Okay!' he spluttered. ''kay won't do it again.'

Off in the distance, sirens howled.

Mike looked over at Bernice. 'Did you hit a screamer button?'

'Yeah!' she looked at the fairy. 'Wasn't expecting that sort of help.'

'Lady?' Mike bowed to the fairy. 'The local authorities are coming to correct this youth. Would you retire? Satisfied that your priestesses are now safe.'

The fairy nodded. She dissolved into a puddle that flowed back into the machine, leaving the slimy starch behind.

'Priestess, hey?' Colleen patted the top of the fairy-infested machine with appreciation. 'You know what? I'm gonna tell head office that some of our customers got allergies to the new powder. We don't want to lose good customers.'

Two policemen in body armor burst into the launderette. The youth on the floor crawled across. He grabbed at a policeman's leg and wrapped himself around it.

'They got monsters here,' he said. 'A big slime monster that turned

50

into tinkabell. Yer gotta get me outa here.'

'It's all right. You're coming with us. You can sit in the safety of our lovely cells,' said one policeman. 'Guaranteed monster free.'

He lifted the youth to his feet and led him out of the launderette.

The other bent and looked at the knife. 'Does this belong to the young man?'

'Yeah,' said Colleen. She tugged at the neckline of her housecoat. 'Look what he done to my fwoat.'

The man took out a digital camera and photographed the cut. 'You'll need to get that seen at A&E. We'll need a report sent to our station. Now, monsters?'

'All I know,' said Colleen. 'Is that lad 'tacked me.'

Bernice lifted a hand. 'I hit the screamer button, when this young man distracted that boy by stepping in to help. Then the knife-wielding maniac dropped to the floor rabbiting on about monsters.'

'Bet 'cha it's drugs,' said Colleen.

Mike waited until the police had gone. Then he turned back to the women and handed them a business card. 'If you ever need to replace that machine contact this address. We can help you transfer ... your guest ... safely.'

'Wouldn't she be happier in a country stream?' asked Bernice.

'Water creatures like her are tied to their spring of origin. When the Victorians buried the streams of London to produce the sewer system she was trapped. She would die if we tried to move her away.'

'Who are yer, anyway?' demanded Colleen.

'Me? I work for the Church of England. I'm a...' He grinned at her. '...I'm an exorcist.'

The Night Café

Yes, it hungers, but tonight it seeks a mate. All things search for one of their own kind. Even Dr Frankenstein provided a mate for his monster.

Jake shuffled around on the barstool so that he could see the pub entrance. She was late, that was very unlike her. A few people were having after-work beers before heading home. Jake ran a hand through his hair and stuffed the last of his crisps in his mouth. Gulping a mouthful of beer to wash them down, he impatiently watched the door.

It opened and Jake sat up eagerly. But only a group of six men walked in.

Over the hum of the sports channel on the TV Jake heard, 'My round first.'

The man dumped a large gym bag at a table. The others dropped similar bags on top. One reached a stool from another table and joined the rest. Jake watched the round-buyer. His dark brown hair was gathered into a plait that fell to his waist and a beard shadowed his chin. The other men in the group wore their hair shoulder-length gathered back into ponytails. They were an odd looking bunch, sort of like academic hippies, but they gave Jake something to look at while he waited for Alice.

Long Plait walked to the bar, while the others settled on their plush covered seats.

'You're just lucky the Umpire ruled in your favor, Kilbride. You were definitely Out.'

Kilbride, on the borrowed stool, shook his head. 'My bat touched crease just a millisecond before Karl knocked the bails from the stumps.'

'So say you,' said the man at the bar. Absently, he stroked a metal decoration on the edge of the bar. 'I can't say it would have been convenient for you to go Out then.'

A chink of glass cut through the rapid commentary as he picked up the first three pint glasses and brought them to the table. Jake watched Kilbride run the back of his hand over the metal leg of the table. Then, before he could wonder why, an arm wrapped around his shoulders.

'Hi, Jake,' said Alice. She snuggled into his neck.

'I didn't see you come in,' he said.

'You weren't here when I arrived, so I went to the ladies to freshen up. God! What have you done to your hair?'

Jake looked in the mirror behind the bar and saw that when he'd run a hand through it he'd forgotten that he had used styling gel earlier; it stuck up in odd spikes.

Alice giggled and rummaged in the hunter-gatherer sack she called a handbag. She produced a comb and held it out.

'You do it, make me look pretty,' said Jake, reaching for his wallet. 'What are you having?'

Alice tutted but re-styled his hair flat.

'I'll have a...'

She looked in the bar mirror. Jake could have sworn she went white. She dumped the comb in her bag and buried her face in his neck again.

Distracted by affection he said, 'You'll have a...?'

'Do you know,' said Alice, her breath tickled his ear. 'I'm not really in the mood for a pub, tonight. Can we go somewhere else?'

'That'll be great.' Jake's eyes lit up. 'I know a great restaurant across the Common. I'm hungry, how about you?'

'Across the Common?' Alice drew back slightly. 'Can we go to somewhere nearer?'

He drained his pint. Stomach full for a moment, he kissed her cheek. 'I was up there earlier. I know which tracks to avoid, since I set up all the warn-offs.'

Alice frowned. 'I suppose it's okay, but didn't you say that the only thing they found from the last girl was her handbag?'

'You're safe with me, sweetheart.'

'Yeah,' said Alice, tucking her hand into his. 'That's the nice thing about dating a cop.'

Alice snuggled up to his right side as they passed the cricketers. The man who had bought the round looked up from savoring his Real Ale as Jake brushed the table.

'So which of the fifth years will pass, do you say Dunkley?'

The man turned back to his group.

She grants the opportunity. She must know and desire a joining. Soon it will share the hunger.

London was never really dark; a warm orange glow flooded the streets. Jake directed Alice to one side of the pub entrance and hauled her into a kiss. She leaned against him.

He backed off, just a little. 'I'm hungry--aren't you? It's a fair hike.'

'Depends on what for,' said Alice nuzzling his lips again.

She must have felt his withdrawal and rummaged in her bag. 'I've got a cereal bar. Here take it. Are you doing house to house? This case is really giving you lots of exercise. You're always hungry these days.'

She hitched her bag over her shoulder again and gripped his hand, starting towards the Common.

Jake ripped open the wrapper and hoovered up the snack.

Above them, the moon lit up the dark, iron gateway. There were a few white lights on the Common, if you stuck to the paths.

Jake released her hand and tucked an arm around her shoulder.

'Did you recognize those men in the pub?' he asked.

'How like a policeman, always asking questions,' said Alice.

'That's a put off,' he said.

Alice slipped her hand around his waist. 'A girl's got to have some secrets.'

'Fine! So how was work today?' he asked.

She shrugged. 'Pretty much the same as usual. Full of stupid people who want my boss to sort out all their problems by magic--and for free.'

The walked on for a bit, out of the light of the last streetlamp, but not yet into the circle cast by the next one.

He took a breath. 'Do you believe in magic, Alice? Real magic?'

Alice pulled out from his grip, walked a few steps, turned and stared at him, unsmiling. 'And where is this going?'

Stunned by her reaction he said, 'Hey babe, what's wrong?'

He stepped forward to reach her, but she stepped back. She put her hands on her hips. He noticed her right hand was very close to her bag. He suspected, but took care never to know officially, that she carried mace or pepper gas--most sensible women did.

'I want to know what you mean by that question. It's not something that I would normally get asked on a date.'

He shifted his gaze from her penetrating stare. 'It's just that sometimes we get these... odd bodies and the detectives pick up a card and just by looking at the card they declare them to be an accident. How anyone can accidentally...'

Alice jumped in. 'Forget it all. Never even think about them. Pretend that you never learned about them.' She turned away from him but he caught her whisper. 'I wish I had the chance to stay ignorant.'

Alice hugged her coat around her and walked away.

She's going! Don't let her go! She knows. She will want revenge.

He ran after her. 'Hey, I'm sorry, babe. You've had a bad time, haven't you?' He pulled her down onto a bench and held her tight. After a while he nuzzled her neck She leant into the caress and turned her face for a kiss that lasted.

He looked around. The Common was empty. He stood, pulling Alice to her feet, and tugged her off the path.

'Come on,' he said, breathlessly.

Alice balked. 'No! I can't. Not here. You never know who might be out with a camera.'

'You've been reading too many tabloids. There's no one here.' He leant forwards and kissed her again, leading her off the path. 'It's safe, you're with me.'

'You don't understand,' said Alice. 'If we got caught and police looked me up... well it could be the end of your career.'

'Don't be silly.'

'I changed my name to Carsden a year or so ago.' She took a deep breath. 'I'm a brat packer.'

'A what?'

'My dad, well he's not my real dad, but my mum married a Glam Rocker when I was a year old. So he's been my dad. I just want to be ordinary. Anyway you said you were hungry.' She stepped back to the path. He caught her wrist and spun her to face him.

'I've got a different hunger now. No one will catch us.' He tugged on her hand. 'But you are going to come up with a translation for that.'

'Yeah, over dinner, later.'

'Over dinner,' he said. He tugged her hand again and nodded into the darkness.

Alice glanced up and down the path. There was no one in sight. She looked at him shyly. She leant forwards and pecked his lips.

'If you really want to, I suppose it's dark enough.'

His face lit up. Grabbing both her hands Jake pulled Alice towards some trees. 'I know just the spot.'

'You bring all the girls here?' said Alice, primly but her eyes danced.

'I only have eyes for you,' he said.

They reached the shadow of the trees. He grabbed her and pulled her tightly to him.

Against his lips she said, 'Now why did I know you'd say that?'

He pulled her down into some long grass. Alice gave one last guilty glance towards the path. There was still no one about. He slid a hand under her shirt and stroked her firm breast, kissing her deeply.

It seeks a mate and this is the one. With the aid of the grass Jake sees Alice.

Alice watches a man standing on the hillside. Jake knows it just needs a spark. There is no time for the man to run. Jake is quite clear that at this point Alice is unaware that the man is her biological father. The man gazes at her in despair then calmly sets off the explosion.

Jake gasps in almost ecstasy; he can hear Alice's thoughts.

We can have revenge against those who sent him.
No! This happened a long time ago.
Revenge takes a long time to brew.

Alice jumped to her feet, her shirt hanging open. 'Jake get off that patch of grass, quickly!'

'Why Alice? Come back down here, you look so sexy like that.'

'There's something wrong here.'

'It's just your nerves about open-air sex.'

He reached for her leg to pull her back down. She backed away.

'Oh God! It's already got you. You brought me here.'

'I need you, Alice.'

Alice continued backing away. He could see the moonlight glinting in her fear-wide eyes.

'What are you?' she whispered.

'I was on one of those weird murder cases,' he said, crawling towards her. 'Then I sat down for my lunch and just got hungrier and hungrier the more I ate. Join with it and then we can be hungry together.'

'What have you been eating?'

'Anything I could,' he said.

'Those missing women?' she said.

'I can't help it, Alice.' He got to his feet and strolled to stand between her and the path. 'I'm so hungry.'

'Stay away from me.' Her hand dropped into her bag. 'Just stay back.'

'Hey babe, everyone wants someone like them. Come back here.'

Alice sprinted into the trees. Jake dashed after her. Low branches lashed at his face.

'Alice!' he called. 'Don't run off like that. It's not safe on your own.'

She must join. Either that or she must never be found.
~No! I love her.
She will tell. She will destroy us.

Burning spray hit his eyes and lungs.

He clawed at his face.

Alice brushed past him. He tried to grab her.

Through watering eyes he saw her heading back the way they had come. Back towards the path and she had her mobile out.

She is going to tell.
~No! Alice!

'No! Alice.' He staggered after her, trying to get to the phone, before it answered.

'Please, answer quickly,' he heard her say.

'Alice! If you don't join with me.' His eyes began to clear as it mended the pain. 'I'll have to eat you. I don't want to lose you. You are everything to me.'

'Alasdair,' she shouted into the phone. 'He's trying to eat me.'

Jake ripped the phone from her hand. 'You said you didn't have a boyfriend.'

'I don't! You're my boyfriend. You were.' She backed away.

Jake lunged. He caught her elbow and hauled her close enough to yell in her face. 'So who's Alasdair?' He shook the phone.

Alice jerked her knee up, as a cop Jake expected it and twisted his hips. He didn't expect her to stamp her heel on his instep. He howled.

As his hands loosened their grip, Alice rammed her knee up.

Jake dropped to the ground. She had only got his thigh, but that was close enough.

Alice fled into the dark.

A male voice at the other end of the phone said, 'Alice? Alice Carsden?'

Jake flung the phone into the bushes. Scrambling painfully to his feet, he lunged after her.

He felt tears running down his face.

Take her, or take her down.
~No! Alice!

'Alice,' he begged. 'Don't make me eat you. I'm so hungry. I just wanted someone to share the hunger with.'

He heard her trip and scramble to her feet. She was backed against the tree, where he had set his trap. He walked towards her. If he could keep her on the grass until the curse had worked.

'Alice, I love you.'

She lifted her hand. She held her comb in her hand. She wound it once with grass.

'Bind!' she shouted.

She twisted another link.

'Bind!' she said again.

The hunger inside him recognized the spell. 'No! Alice! Stop that!'

Run! Run!

Jake stopped edging towards her and tried to back away; his feet felt so heavy. Alice wrapped the strand of grass around the comb, with his hair glued to it with styling gel, for the third time.

'BIND!' she shouted out.

57

He tried to run.

His feet were rooted to the spot.

He could see tears leaking down her face, tears that matched his own.

'Let me go Alice. Join with me.'

Voice quivering she said, 'You chose the wrong victim this time. Did I know the men in the pub? You're going to wish I didn't.'

She tried to pull away. Her eyes opened wide in fear again.

'No! I left my own hairs on the comb as well.'

Jake and the hunger grinned; she was as bound to the grass as he was.

Join with us, taste the hunger. You can be revenged on those who killed your father.

'My father chose to die to save me.'

Again Jake could hear her thoughts. The man was driven to it in desperation. You could have got to know him, to live with him.

'My father died to save me!' She spoke as if by rote.

'Alice I love you,' said Jake. 'Join with us, it'll just be like marriage. You want to be married don't you?'

'Get it out of my head,' whispered Alice. 'If you love me, let me go!'

Eat her, whispered the hunger. You'll have to eat her. She will never join with us. She doesn't understand anything.

~NO! Alice!

'Alice! Please understand Alice, I don't want to eat you. Join with us.

'NO!' Alice screamed. 'Stop it!'

'ALICE! Where are you?' called a male voice from the woods. Jake recognized it as Alasdair from the phone.

'ALICE!'

'Alasdair!' Alice shouted. 'Help!'

The crashing through the trees was more than one man.

Six men burst into the clearing. Three carried swords, one a big spear with a cross piece just below the blade and the other two held guns.

The man with the spear charged over to Alice. 'What happened?'

'I bound myself here when I bound him. Get me out of here! It's trying to take me too!'

Alasdair gestured to another of the gunmen. The other four stood in a loose ring around the glade.

The hunger inside him made Jake twist his neck and try to bite the newcomer, but the spell Alice had used bound his whole body.

'Dunkley?' Jake recognized the one called Kilbride in the pub. 'How are they held?'

'She's a witch,' snapped Jake. 'She cast a spell on me.'

Dunkley, the one Alice called Alasdair, smiled slightly. 'She's not.' He turned to Alice. 'I somehow doubt you changed your mind and actually joined a coven. They would have taught you not to bind yourself into the spell.'

'Oh, you can just see the headlines, can't you?' Alice said. 'Steven Stempress's step-daughter in devil worshipping cult.'

'Most of them aren't like that.'

'Yes, and how many times have you read the phrase *so-called white witch*?'

'Too many times,' Dunkley said. 'When I pull you off the grass it will break the dual binding. Be ready, Kilbride.'

Alasdair pulled her away from Jake. The binding broke as he strained to reach his girl.

Run! screamed the hunger.

Jake braced to run.

Kilbride tackled him and brought him down across the patch of grass.

'He tried to make me like him, and when I felt what was happening, he tried to eat me.' Alice's voice only quivered a little. 'God! Do I have *victim* painted on my forehead? In neon nail varnish?'

'Because of your history, you will remain a victim until you choose to learn how to protect yourself.' Dunkley crouched and stared Jake in the eyes. 'I can help you. I can fill the hunger. Will you come with us?'

'Please!' Tears fell down. 'I'm so hungry. I just need something to eat.'

'What is it?' Alice stood in the shadows. She fastened her blouse and tucked it into her trousers.

'It's a hungry ghost. It usually enters a victim by hungry grass.'

'That patch of grass he's lying on. That's how I... I bound him to it,' said Alice.

Dunkley produced a torch from his pocket and shone it on the grass. Jake could feel the grass trying to shrink away from the brilliance. He needed to eat again. He was wasting away as if something was eating him from the inside. The torch shone into his face, but stayed away from his eyes.

'What can you do for him?' asked Alice.

'Nothing tonight,' Dunkley said rubbing at his beard. 'We'll take him into the college and house him in a penitent's cell. Then come back and sort out the grass tomorrow.'

'Hey! I'm here you know!' said Jake. Around him, the other four men stood in a guard position: not that there was anyone to keep away.

'No,' said Alice, not looking at him. 'It's not you in there. You can't leave this here. This is clearly a...'

'Lover's trysting place?' Dunkley said, amused.

Jake watched Kilbride jerk his head up at the tone in Dunkley's voice.

Kilbride looked between Alice and Dunkley, speculation on his face.

Jake snarled. That tone of voice had been very fond.

'You're supposed to be the great all-powerful wizard. Why can't you do something now?' said Alice.

'I'm not a wizard.'

'Oh come on!' said Alice. 'I've read up on you. You're the Wizard-Smiths in a modern form.

Kilbride stepped closer and lowered his voice.

'This lady seems to know a lot about us,' he said. 'And she bound him, the way we would...'

Dunkley gave a half smile. 'Sorry, Kilbride, I forgot to introduce you. This is Alice Carsden.'

'Carsden?' Kilbride clearly recognized the name. 'I'm sorry, Miss Carsden. I trained with Gordon.' He thought for moment, then added, 'She's right, you know, if it's not dealt with tonight someone's going to have to stand watch here, all night.'

'That's what fourth years are for,' Dunkley said.

Kilbride grinned. 'You could show Miss Carsden how to banish the hungry grass, if she has enough strength. You've suggested before, to the Council, how we ought to teach women.'

Dunkley nodded towards one of the other men. 'Marishes would snitch on me.'

'We can send the others off to search this area for more problems,' said Kilbride.

'But why can't you do it yourself?' Alice demanded.

Kilbride grinned from his position holding down the struggling Jake. 'We all grounded out our strength before we started drinking. Alcohol and power...'

'Strength,' insisted Dunkley.

Kilbride shrugged. 'Strength then. Alcohol and strength don't mix well.'

Dunkley studied Alice. 'Hmmm?'

'Are you sure I could?' said Alice. 'I mean all I usually do is keep my coffee warm at work'

Dunkley shrugged. 'Kilbride's correct. You have the strength to perform the banishment--you must have been warming your coffee fairly regularly.'

Alice looked away, the way she did to hide a blush when he caught her lying. Jake normally found it adorable.

'Alice,' he snarled. 'You're not going to believe them?'

She glared at him, then turned back to Dunkley and snapped, 'Fine, show me what to do.'

Dunkley gestured the other men closer. 'We need to search this area. There may be other patches of Hungry Grass about. Kilbride I'll need you to guard my back to make sure we don't get spectators.'

The other four men slid away into the darkness.

He will use her to kill you.

'Don't kill me,' said Jake. 'Alice, he's going to get you to kill me.'

Alice shook her head. 'We're going to make you well again.'

Dunkley unscrewed the shaft of his spear.

'That blade length is illegal,' said Jake.

'I have a license to carry it, as do all these men,' answered Dunkley. He crouched and put the collapsed spear into his gym bag. 'We each also hold a firearms license. It's necessary in our job. As a policeman, you will have met the calling cards we leave behind. We deal with problems, like you. Alice do you have any silver on you?'

Alice shook her head.

Dunkley unfastened his shirt collar, hauled a crucifix over his head and tossed it to Alice.

Her hand shook as she reached for the chain.

Jake watched as she dropped it over her head and tucked it under her shirt. He growled in his throat. He could almost feel the warmth of the chain against her breast.

'Kilbride will hold him physically, because you will have to concentrate on the banishment. Both on this man and the grass, together. You'll need to drive the spirit out of him and bind it to the grass, then you must burn the grass.' Dunkley rubbed his beard again. 'You know to concentrate on a the result, using a focus of words to direct your intent?'

Alice nodded. 'I can do that. I... Me and Penny, we...'

'Don't be afraid,' Kilbride said. 'I'll keep him off you.'

She looked at Jake. The quarter moon was enough to see tears standing in her eyes. 'I used to love Jake. Why did you take him?'

'Alice this is Jake in here,' he replied.

She turned away. 'I'm ready.'

'Do you need the mnemonics that I use?' asked Dunkley.

'No, but I'll need a knife.' Jake noticed that Alice's voice was thin.

61

Dunkley bent and pulled a dirk from his sock. He handed it to Alice. He held her gaze for a moment.

Alice reached for the knife, then smiled. She withdrew her hand and took a penny from her pocket and held it out to him.

'A gift to prevent the cutting of friendship,' he said, taking the coin.

Alice looked like she was trying to drink in the man's calm attitude as she took the knife.

They're going to kill you. Take her hostage.
~Alice!

'Alice! They're going to kill me.'

Alice rubbed her eyes, then looked straight in his face.

Alice held out the comb. Using the knife she cut the grass that wound around the teeth.

Run! Run!
~I'm so hungry.

'I'm so hungry,' Jake said. 'Alice, I'm hungry.'

He kicked backwards, but the hands held him in place. If only he could roll and put this Kilbride in contact with the grass. He had to get Free, he had to run. He struggled under the man's weight.

Alice knelt beside him. She laid her hands on his forehead. 'Get out!'

Her hands burnt. He felt her reaching inside his skull and dragging his brain out, piece by piece.

He screamed. 'Alice!'

'Get out!'

He writhed under the burning hands. His whole body was alight. The hunger burnt in his stomach. He could feel it clawing its way up his throat. It ate his vocal cords, until he could no longer scream.

'Thrice I say Get Out!' Alice's voice was strangely calm.

He coughed.

Kilbride rolled off him.

Free, he got to his knees. He tried to get on his feet. He had to run.

The burning hands lifted from his forehead. His stomach pushed. Coughing and retching, the Hunger crawled out of Jake. It poured out of his mouth onto the grass.

His arms quivered and Dunkley pulled him aside before he fell face first into the vomit.

Alice stood and lifted her hands above her head. 'Burn! Burn! Burn!' she shrieked.

Looking up at her, Jake saw a marble angel appealing to heaven for salvation.

The grass burst into blue-hot flames. The acrid stench of burning vomit filled the air.

Alice sank to her knees, looking like she was about to faint.

Dunkley slipped handcuffs over Jake's wrist. 'You are in custody, to account for your actions re: the murder of seven women on this Common.'

Jake felt empty. There was nothing left. He had thrown up his whole self.

Kilbride knelt beside Alice. He held a bottle of lucozade to her lips, and she gulped it.

His head was empty. His Soul was empty. He stared into empty space. There was no joy left.

He opened his mouth and screamed.

Sin Not by Silence

Mr. Edwards tugged on the door again. The resistance was unusual--the time-blackened oak was balanced to swing open at a touch.

He pulled harder. Entering as he had via the vestry door, he still needed to check the path up to the main entrance hadn't been used as repository for second hand pizza and curry from the Friday night clubbers.

Gradually, the door swung in.

A hand was clenched on the handle. Mr. Edwards jerked back. For a moment he thought the unkempt man clinging to the handle was dead, but the man opened feral, gray eyes.

A movement along the path jerked his head up from the sight at his feet. A young red-haired man walked out of the lychgate with his head bowed. An older man with a long plait hanging to his waist had an unfriendly hand on the younger man's shoulder, escorting him.

Mr. Edwards nearly called out to them but the man in the church porch grabbed the cloth of his surplice. Their shadowy forms were lost the morning fog, which was creeping back to the river in fear of the sun.

'Please,' the man whispered, hoarsely. 'I swear I'll never do it again. Forgive me?'

Horrified by the man's poor state, Mr. Edwards lifted him by his elbow.

'This is the place for forgiveness, come in.'

The man's clothes looked like knives had ripped them or, looking at the parallel scores, maybe claws had cut through the cloth.

'I'll never do it again,' begged the man, shuffling along while clinging to Mr. Edwards.

'You're safe now.' Mr. Edwards led him towards the altar. 'Perhaps you could tell me how you came to be here?'

* * * *

Crouching in the darkness, Felbridge watched the man creep through the undergrowth of the common. The moonlight glinted on a long knife--actually, on looking closer, it was a sword--in the man's hand. The swordsman hunted one who strolled among the trees.

Felbridge barely kept his hand from shaking as he remembered the body last night. He gritted his teeth to keep his snarl of rage un-vocalized as he remembered the man almost ripped apart by a long knife. The tarmac under him had been stained with more blood then he thought a body held. And the victim had left a long streak of red along the road as he tried to crawl away.

While the swordsman focused on his prey, Felbridge sprinted up and leapt on his back.

'Police!' shouted Felbridge. 'You'll not cut anymore people.'

The swordsman rolled over and backhanded Felbridge in the teeth.

'Stupid idiot,' hissed the swordsman.

Despite the strength of the blow, Felbridge clung on. 'You're not getting away this time.'

From up on the hill came the sound of someone running it terror.

'He's away now,' said the swordsman. He let the sword drop in to the grass. 'You can let me go, now you've warned the murderer that we're after him.'

'Oh no! You're not getting me that way,' said Felbridge. 'Who are you?'

'If you'll let me retrieve my ID, I think you'll better understand the enormity of what you have just done.'

'Hold out your wrists. I'll see ID at the station.'

The swordsman stared at Felbridge, as if he thought the policeman had gone mad. His gaze ran over the bruise starting on Felbridge's face.

With a heavy sigh the swordsman clasped his hands in front of him. Felbridge fastened the cuffs around his wrists.

'Just bring the sword, will you?' said the swordsman. 'I don't want to have to come back looking for it in all these bushes.'

'Of course I'm bringing the sword--it's evidence,' said Felbridge. Using gloved hands he retrieved the blade from the ground and marched its owner towards his car.

* * * *

'Here, take a drink,' said Mr. Edwards.

He offered water offered in a flower vase, which Mr. Edwards had fetched from the vestry.

The penitent gulped the water down, not disdaining the poor cup.

* * *

Once in the light of the station, the swordsman said, 'Right if you'll just take out my wallet, top pocket, you'll find a business card. I think you'll be more understanding.'

Felbridge reached in. He opened the wallet. In one of the side pockets of the wallet was a white card. He froze as he saw the plain red cross printed across the left corner. There was nothing else on the card. He flicked a glance at the man in front of him.

Felbridge remembered the last time he'd seen one of these cards--

they were usually found on a very messily dead body.

'Who are you?' demanded Felbridge. 'An assassin?'

'Has no one explained these cards to you?' the man looked puzzled.

'Of course,' spat Felbridge. 'We're to accept there is no solving the case. Well, not this time, sunshine, I'm going to find out what's going on here.'

* * * *

The penitent bent over. His forehead nearly touched his knees as he knelt before the altar. 'I've been such a damned fool.'

The vicar rested a gentle hand on his shoulders. 'Tell me it all.'

* * * *

The man's fancy mobile trilled and Felbridge snatched it up. He hit the answer key.

'I'll take that, please,' said the swordsman.

Felbridge ignored him. He listened to a strained voice sounded on the other end.

'Dunkley? What happened? I thought you were going to get him tonight?'

'My name is Detective Felbridge. I have a man here in interview that has been arrested for attempted murder.'

'What? Are you insane? What station? Oh, you're in real trouble.' The phone went dead without Felbridge even telling the man on the other end where the station was.

There was a look of malicious amusement in the swordsman's eyes as he stared at Felbridge.

Two minutes later the Superintendent was in the interview room.

'Felbridge! What the hell have you done? I've just had the Chief Constable on the phone demanding that I release this man.'

'I caught him stalking someone with a sword.'

The chief turned to the sword man, who stood up. The cuffs dropped off, open. They clattered on the floor, sounding large in the strained atmosphere.

'Thank you for vouching for me, sir,' said the man quietly.

A tall blond man burst into the room followed by younger red-haired man who carried a gym bag.

'Dunkley what happened here?' asked the blond.

'I attempted to identify myself, but was refused release.' His brown eyes burned with angry fire. 'Who was killed tonight, Trewithick?'

'A young woman,' Trewithick said, his voice expressionless. 'She was on her way home from her twenty-first birthday party.'

Both men turned looks of hatred on Felbridge. The Chief joined them.

'But I stopped him...'

'You stopped me from taking the killer into custody,' Dunkley said. A gravelly Scots accent was marked as he whispered, 'For each night he stays uncaptured, he will kill. Every person who dies will have been killed by you.'

Felbridge's mouth dropped open as he stared in horror at the man he had brought in for questioning.

'I lay this on your soul,' Dunkley said, quietly. 'I take from you the protection of the church...'

'Dunkley! No!' Trewithick said.

'He deserves...'

'For your soul's sake no!'

Dunkley's hands clenched. 'For twenty-four hours then, you are without our protection.' He swung around on his colleague and hissed, 'And don't push it any further.'

'He won't last an hour.'

'Then he'll learn why we exist.'

The redhead stared between the two older men. He turned to look at Felbridge and his eyes opened wide. 'Sir, that's...'

Dunkley glared at him and he silenced.

'After a full day,' continued Dunkley he checked his watch. 'At 3am tomorrow morning, if you are still alive go to a church and confess your sin and beg the forgiveness of the vicar. I will try and rectify your mistake.'

Grabbing his sword, he stormed out of the room. The chief turned to Felbridge.

'You are suspended pending an investigation,' said the chief. He too left.

Trewithick tried to leave but the young red head grabbed his sleeve. 'Sir, we can't leave him unprotected like this. He's...' He paused. 'He's marked, sir.'

'That's what Dunkley intended.'

'And you allow this?'

'Rules are meant to protect, not restrict, Josh, but they do need to be followed.'

'At least we can to escort him to the safety of his home.'

Trewithick shook his head. 'Dunkley has removed our protection.'

'Then I'll do it myself,' Josh said. He stared Trewithick straight in the eyes. The older man sighed.

'I can't let you do that,' Trewithick said.

'You can't stop me.'

'I meant, I can't let you do that alone. I'd better help.' Trewithick turned to Felbridge. 'We'll take you now.'

Confused, Felbridge followed the two men.

Before opening the door Trewithick reached into his gym bag. He produced a walking stick and drew from it a sword.

'That's illegal,' said Felbridge.

Trewithick cast a scornful glance at him. 'You're in no position to comment.' He tossed his gym bag to Josh who pulled out another sword. He unsheathed it, dropping the sheath back into the bag. He shrugged the bag on his back and nodded firmly at Trewithick.

'You and Dunkley! God save me from any more stubborn Northerners,' muttered Trewithick as he nodded to Josh to pull open the door.

Felbridge licked his lips. He wondered what they thought would be waiting.

There was nothing on the other side, and Felbridge was inclined to laugh at their posturing. 'For a minute there you had me going.'

'Shut up,' Josh said. 'You don't know how much trouble you're in.'

They walked through the outer office and reception area. Most people acted as if the three men weren't there, but one or two...

The reception desk clerk opened wide horrified eyes as she saw him. She turned her head and he saw tears leaking from under her hand.

Officer Gladders, whom Felbridge knew to be a good beat patroller, darted his tongue in, which had just started to hang out. He watched Felbridge with hungry eyes. The beat officer's watchful gaze followed him to the main entrance, but they flicked to the two men carrying swords.

'Right,' Trewithick said. 'We'll go in my van. It's got enough wards on it that we might not leave a trail to your house.'

'But what about my car?' said Felbridge.

Trewithick bit his tongue on the words he clearly wanted to say. 'Give Josh your keys, he can follow us to your house. Josh stay here with him. I'll get the van.'

* * * *

'I killed her,' whispered the penitent. 'She was only twenty-one and I killed her.' He gulped the air like a drowning man.

Mr. Edwards nodded. 'Yes, I can see that. Yet you are here.'

* * * *

'And stay put,' Trewithick said. 'Don't answer the door, or the telephone, or turn on the television or your computer. Those are all means by which they can gain entry to your home.'

Trewithick turned to go.

Josh stood by the van. 'Sir, you don't live near the college, could you drop me at the nearest tube station?'

'Of course.'

Both men got in the van and Felbridge watched them drive off. He closed the door, slowly. Then he locked it and fastened the double bolts. He turned on all the lights and sat in his chair staring at the off television.

As dawn began to creep through the windows, Felbridge shook off his unreasoning awe. It was all nonsense. He pulled his coat on. He was hungry and decided to get a curry from the shop on the corner, which would be still open.

As he touched the first dead bolt, panic coiled in his stomach. He shook his head. He wasn't going to let any idiots frighten him. Firmly he pulled back the bolt and the second, and unlocked the door. He stepped out onto the pavement and strolled through the growing light.

Someone came out of an alleyway between two shops. Felbridge jumped back, heart pounding, then he relaxed.

'Hello Mr Felbridge,' said Officer Gladders. He fell into step beside Felbridge darting glances at him. 'I was sorry to hear about your suspension, sir.'

'I'm sure it will all come out okay,' said Felbridge. 'I'm just going for a curry.' Gladders shrugged. His eyes searched the street with a frenzied intensity. Felbridge watched him then checked the street himself.

They were alone.

'What's with the eagle eyes?' Felbridge paused. 'I didn't know you were on this beat.'

'I'm not.' Gladders slammed a hand over Felbridge's mouth and had his wrist twisted behind him in a grip like a clamp. 'You see Mr. Felbridge you're fair game, and I want to hunt.'

There was a sexual intensity to the heavy breathing in Felbridge's ear. The pain in his arm buckled his knees, but Gladders dragged him back into the alley where he had been waiting.

Then it hit Felbridge. There was something ... not entirely natural about Gladders's strength.

'I waited, I thought you might come out in daylight, you see. And there's no one who will gainsay me my prize.'

Felbridge tried to bite the hand over his mouth, but Gladders laughed--a high mad sound.

Until he was backhanded across the cheek. A blow that sent him skidding across to alley to thud against the yard gate of one of the terrace houses.

'Wrong, boggle.'

Josh held the sword in his left hand, his right clothed in a set of black knuckle-dusters.

Felbridge scrambled behind Josh and got warily to his feet.

'But he's fair game,' whimpered Gladders patting at what looked like a burn around his face where the knuckle-dusters had hit him. 'You're not playing fair.'

'Life's not fair,' parroted Josh. He backed into Felbridge.

'Thanks,' said Felbridge. Nodding at the knuckle-dusters he added, 'Those don't look like brass.'

'Iron,' Josh said. 'We make our own equipment. I thought we told you to stay home.'

Gladders bared sharp jagged teeth. 'He's my prize.'

'Run!' shouted Josh. Dragging on Felbridge's arm, he sprinted out of the alleyway.

Felbridge needed no further encouragement. He fled up the pavement, his coat flying out around him like a shadow. From every corner he saw eyes staring at him hungrily. Just behind him, Josh kept pace.

Felbridge fumbled out his keys and skidded to a halt on his step. He rammed the key in the lock and shoved open the door. He held it for Josh but Josh stayed outside.

'Don't invite *anyone* in,' reproved Josh. 'I might not be me, if you know what I mean. I'll wait out here. At 3 a.m., we'll try and get you a church.'

'Why not wait until dawn?'

'Because in the hours before dawn they will attack and break into your house, just to get you.' Josh stepped back and hid the sword under his anorak. 'Be ready at 3 a.m.'

* * * *

'Those things, what are they?' Tears ran down his cheeks now.

'Leftovers from a darker time,' said Mr. Edwards. 'The worst of their kind, they were driven onto these Isles to protect the rest of the world. Our Night Watchmen, the Vigilae, are all that stands between their dominion, and us.'

* * * *

Josh leaned against the wall nearby. He nodded curtly to Felbridge. He straightened and tugged his anorak straight. 'Let's get going then.'

Felbridge hovered in the doorway his hand clenched around a kitchen knife in his pocket. 'Show me your hand.'

Josh lifted his hands. Neither of them carried the knuckle-duster.

With his other hand, Felbridge produced a baseball bat from behind his back.

'Very good,' Josh said. He slipped his hand into his own pocket and the iron weapon was back on his hand. 'Maybe you are worth saving.'

Felbridge stepped out of the door and pulled it shut. He heard the lock catch like a nail hammered into his coffin.

'Why are you doing this?'

'Because you made a mistake,' Josh said. 'M'tutors are always going on about how we need to give everyone a second chance. So I'm going to try and give you yours.'

'You're defying that top guy!'

Josh shrugged as he slipped the sword from under his anorak. 'Even Caesar had a slave to whisper in his ear, "Th'art mortal, Caesar."'

'So how long have you done this job?' asked Felbridge, impressed by the familiarity that Josh showed handling the sword.

'I've been in training for less than a year,' admitted Josh. 'The apprenticeship is for seven.'

Felbridge nearly ran back home, but he was sure that Josh was his only hope.

Together they paced between the street lamps, which held the night at bay with pools of orange light.

'I thought you said you were going back to your college,' said Felbridge. He squinted through the curtains of fog that crept up from the river, isolating the islands of sight.

'No,' Josh said, his eyes scanning every corner and shadow. 'I asked for a lift to the nearest tube station, at no point did I say I was going back to college. I was quite careful about that. '

'Ah! Can't we run?' asked Felbridge.

'No,' Josh said. He seemed to watching from the corner of his eyes. Sometimes he sniffed the air like a dog. Sometimes he tilted his head as if listening to a sound above Felbridge's hearing.

'Why? Do they sense fear?' muttered Felbridge.

Josh peered at him. 'I suppose, but we're going to have to run for it in a bit. And I think we should save your strength for then. You're twitching--wasting energy.'

Josh sniffed and spun as Gladders rushed out of the shadows. The great sword that Josh carried cut into Gladders's arm. Blood spurted out.

'Now we run,' Josh said. 'Get to the next light.'

With a glance over his shoulder, Felbridge saw two more creatures leap out of the dark. They looked human, but they moved like cats. One of them paused over Gladders. It bent its head, and Felbridge was sure it lapped at the blood as Gladders tried to push it off.

As they ran the next light flickered and died.

* * * *

'Can you forgive me, please?' the penitent clutched at the vicar's surplice.

'It doesn't matter how many times *I* forgive you,' said Mr. Edwards. 'Until *you* forgive you, then God cannot reach into your heart.'

The penitent buried his tears in the vicar's knee. 'But she was only twenty-one. I'll just go and let them kill me.'

'That's not how it works,' said Mr. Edwards, not moving in his seat on the end of a pew. 'You have come here for forgiveness, you are in our care now. That will protect you while you earn your forgiveness.'

'Penance, you mean?'

* * * *

Creatures crowded in from all sides.

Felbridge stumbled as his nightmares took life on the street. Some scuttled like beetles, others had clawed fingers--and they were all human.

Unkempt hair hung from their heads and some wore rags, yet another, a pleasant looking woman, was dressed in a power suit.

He licked his lips. She was hot. He slowed his pace to stare at her. Her scarlet lips parted. He was panting, but not from the run.

A sting slap fell on his cheek. The woman eyes hungered for her lost prey.

'Concentrate,' shouted Josh. 'And whatever you do, don't fall. Once you're down you're dead. Now run!'

Somehow Felbridge got his feet back under him. His thigh stung as claws ripped through the thick cloth of his jogging pants. Not looking, he whacked at the hand with the bat, and kept running.

Josh swung his great sword. It seemed like a fairy blade, trailing starlight with the swing, but the dreadful squishy thunk as it met flesh and bone was very real.

Another critter jumped from the shadows towards Josh's back.

Felbridge took a double-handed hold on his bat and thwacked it in the face.

It skidded across the street.

Horror nearly stopped Felbridge's feet; the creature shook its head and scrambled back to its feet.

It sprang across the road.

Felbridge swung the bat.

The creature opened its maw. Massive saber fangs chomped through the solid wood.

Yanking the splintered end away, Felbridge staggered backwards, then he fled up the street after Josh. Groping in his pocket as he ran, he pulled out the knife--but it slid through his terrified fingers.

The blade clattered on the concrete slabs behind him, but he didn't dare stop to pick it up. Gripping his only weapon, the stump of the bat, he ran.

With a clang, a manhole cover lifted.

Felbridge put on a spurt and jumped down hard on the edge, trapping fingers under the iron edge.

A tortured howl echoed under the dropped drain cover.

Something crouched at the top of the darkened streetlight.

He managed to utter a shriek before it leapt. Felbridge watched the perfect trajectory that would land on his head.

Trying to stop or change direction, his knees buckled. Then that sword of starlight swung.

The head flew over the street thumping on a front door, the rest splattered to the ground. Felbridge skipped over the remains.

'There's the church.' Although they were close, despair filled Felbridge's shout.

Josh nodded. Even he seemed out of breath now. There must be at least twenty of the creeping shadows around them.

Josh hooked his free hand through Felbridge's elbow and heaved him into a fancy porch that someone had put out over their step. Swinging the sword discouraged the critters from coming closer.

'What are these things?' asked Felbridge.

'People,' spat Josh.

'Nonsense.'

'They're people who whimper and say, "The spirit possessing me makes me do these awful things."'

Felbridge stared at Josh. 'But you don't believe that, do you?'

Josh snorted. 'The possessing spirit can only suggest--and it suggests what it thinks the person wants to do.'

Felbridge swallowed, out there was beautiful woman in killer-red power suit, a city executive by day, most likely. By night, she was... he shuddered.

While it gave them a breather, holed up as they were on this porch, Felbridge knew they'd never break through the creatures that massed in the shadows to get to the safety. 'Josh, it's me they want--get out if you can.'

'Right!' Josh sneered. 'Just watch this.'

He pulled back.

The creatures surged forward, leaving Felbridge to flail at the creatures with the remains of the baseball bat.

Lifting his sword in both hands, Josh shouted, '*Lux fulgeat!*'

A supernova exploded from the sword. As the flare touched a streetlight it re-ignited. The whole street filled with warmth of daylight.

The creatures with faces from his nightmares scurried back to the shadows.

The sword sagged. Josh's stellar effort had drained him.

Flinging the stump of his bat after the last fleeing creature, Felbridge tucked a hand under Josh's shoulder and tugged him towards the safety of the church.

Panting hard, Josh nodded and picked up the pace.

Behind them the lights began to fade. The padding of paws and the scuffle of claws on concrete paving slabs proved the creatures hadn't left.

Dawn started to burn into the fog as they staggered toward the lychgate into the churchyard.

'We're nearly there,' said Felbridge. 'You've got me here.'

Josh nodded. His strength finally began to return.

The shadow of the lychgate separated and a dark figure scuttled forward.

Josh lifted his sword.

Felbridge stood his ground. There was no point in backing away--nightmares whispered up behind them.

It was a man--sort of. He flexed his long fingers, and claws almost doubled their length. He had long knives on the ends of every finger.

Long knives--that's what the autopsy had said, not swords.

'You're the killer,' he said.

The man grinned, exposing a mouth full of fangs. 'And I thank you. You stopped me being captured last night. Now I know they're on to me, I will move and rest until they have given up the search.'

'No! Josh you've got to get this one.'

Josh shifted his hold on the pommel of his starlit blade and nodded.

'You put so much trust in a baby witchfinder, who is acting against the lore. This one is fair game to my Kind. Stand aside.'

Josh just shook his head. Felbridge had no weapons left. He could neither help, nor protect himself against that which crept up behind.

Josh looked at him. 'Get through the gate and up to the church door. I'll hold them off... as long as I can.'

With a yell, Josh ran at the Knife-fingered man.

Felbridge sprang to one side and sprinted for the gate.

The knife-fingered man grabbed for him. Razor-wire claws sliced through his trousers.

A warm liquid dripped down his shin.

The sword sliced down over an empty space where the knife-fingered man's arm had been. The creature was fast.

It pounced on Josh and Felbridge scrambled to the gate.

From inside the sword's reach, the creature cut at Josh.

Hand on the gate to safety, Felbridge hesitated. Then he turned. In two bounds he was on the knife-fingered man's back, hand-locked around the creature's throat.

Josh stepped back.

The monster was strong, but its claws interfered with its attempts to get a grip and rip Felbridge's hands away. It dropped onto its back, with Felbridge underneath. Its weight bore down on him, crushing the air from his lungs.

Winded, Felbridge's grip slackened. Claws lacerated his finger and he released the creature's neck.

It rolled as Josh's sword almost shaved Felbridge's nose hairs.

Josh pressed the creature against the graveyard wall.

Over his shoulder Josh said, 'Run. Get your hand on the door handle.'

The creature pounced again.

As the rising sun turned the fog into a bloodstained haze, Felbridge saw other creatures slinking towards where he lay on the ground.

Coughing, he rolled and slowly climbed to his feet. He staggered to the gate.

The woman in the red power suit strutted out of the shadow of a nearby shop doorway. With half-lidded eyes, she licked her lips. Behind him he heard the sword clang on the paving slabs and the scrabble of claws.

Felbridge grabbed for the gate latch and backed away, while his body wanted to fall towards her like the pull of gravity.

Her eyes widened in fear--then she was gone. All the creatures of the shadows merged with their home.

Felbridge turned. Barehanded, but still looking like a dark angel, Dunkley charged down the hill.

The knife-fingered creature stumbled away.

Snatching the sword from Josh's hand, Dunkley lifted it high.

'*And the wicked shall quail against the vision of thy majesty!*' he declared.

The sword streamed out the brightest light, but to Felbridge it felt welcoming.

The knife-fingered man cowered against the graveyard wall. Dunkley spun round and face Josh, who clenched his fist.

'Do you think you can stand against me?' asked Dunkley. He flung the still faintly glowing sword over the wall and onto the grass; the point stuck and the handle stood up like a bold cross over a grave, blood and other substances oozed down the blade to burn the grass.

Josh watched it land then he turned back to Dunkley.

'You've got everyone too scared to question you, but I'm too new at this to understand anything but that you are wrong.' Panting for breath Josh added, 'It was a mistake--everyone makes mistakes.'

Dunkley stood motionless on the pavement.

Josh stepped towards him.

For a moment Felbridge was convinced the older man would hit out, but instead he stood aside. Josh turned and grabbed Felbridge. He dragged him through the lychgate, up the path to the safety of the church porch.

'Get the handle, and never let go until the church is opened.'

In the darkness of the porch, Felbridge fumbled about. His knees gave way as the cast iron loop touched his groping finger. Crying with relief, he hugged the handle to his chest.

Looking up he demanded, 'What about you?'

Highlighted against the fading red of the morning fog, Josh shrugged. 'They can only sack me.'

Josh walked down the path.

Dunkley stood, blocking Josh's way out. He held the sword, but with the point down.

'Who made you my conscience?' demanded Dunkley.

Josh's fists clenched. 'That would be my mother. She taught me right from wrong.'

They stood at the lychgate so long that Felbridge imagined them turning to stone in that position. For a moment he had a weird vision that he was seeing the same man at opposite ends of time. Then he felt the door under his hand quiver as the heavy locking bar was removed.

He hung onto the handle.

'Please don't refuse me,' he whispered.

Glancing back at the statues of men, he saw Dunkley nod slightly and hand the sword back to Josh.

'However, I shall escort you to your master to discipline your disobedience.'

Josh bowed his head curtly. As he walked past Dunkley, the older man placed and unfriendly hand on Josh's shoulder.

Vanessa Knipe

The door opened pulling Felbridge inside.

A Coin in the Fountain

Mike walked past an oblivious security guard into the office building and took the lift to the third floor.

Kilbride waited at a door a little way along the corridor.

As Mike walked over to him, the plush carpet hushed the usual clump of his biker boots.

'What's the problem, Kilbride?' Mike asked.

'It's taken me two weeks to get here. Now all leads are gone.' Kilbride ran a hand through his graying hair. 'I need a reading and you're the best at that. Even Dunkley only gets vague impressions.'

Mike shrugged. He followed Kilbride into an office.

A man hunched in his chair. He rocked with his face buried in a tissue.

'I didn't know.' He blew his nose. 'I didn't know. It's not my fault.'

Mike glanced at Kilbride.

Kilbride smiled wryly.

Mike laid his motorcycling helmet and leather biker jacket on the desk.

'Thorby? I need you to explain to my colleague, Mike Rider,' said Kilbride.

The man looked up. His hair stood every which way as the gel fixed the new rough hairstyle.

Mike shifted some papers and sat casually on the desk. 'Go on then, mate, tell me what's happened.'

The sufferer smiled slightly at Mike. 'It's a new website.'

Mike nodded at the screen. 'Call it up for me, will you?'

Thorby scuttled his chair towards the desk. He tossed his tissue in the pile next to the box and shuddered as his hands touched the keys.

'Patrick! What are you doing here?' A woman glided into the room on high heels, carrying some papers.

Both Thorby and Kilbride looked up, guilt passing across their faces.

'Mrs. Glade.' Thorby stopped playing with the keyboard and started flattening his spiky hairdo, all but jumping to his feet like a schoolboy when the headmistress enters.

Using fingertips, she pushed aside Mike's helmet and dropped the papers on the desk, then turned to glare at Mike. Her eyebrows lifted in surprise. Her lips opened slightly as she looked him over. Her eyes lingered over the well-built body shown to advantage by jeans and a white tee shirt. Mike returned the slick brunette's appraisal.

'Hello, Anita,' Kilbride said. He turned to Mike. 'My sister, Anita Glade. Anita, this is my colleague Mike Rider. Anita's the PA to one of the executives here. We're just looking into something. It's not company business so you needn't worry about your balance sheet.'

Mike tried to stop his lip curling into a sneer. If she was Kilbride's sister then she had dyed her hair and was on quantities of botox.

On hearing Kilbride's introduction she turned away from Mike. 'It's highly irregular,' she said. 'I can't see what *you lot* have to investigate here. We're a modern company. No old-fashioned ideas allowed.'

'I'll let you know later, OK?'

She pursed her lips, but glanced at her watch and left the room, giving Kilbride a very meaningful look.

Kilbride smile apologetically at Mike. 'She's still annoyed that I refused to teach her.'

'If Mrs. Glade sees me playing on a non-work thing during office hours,' said Thorby, 'she'll get me sacked.' But he turned back to the computer.

Mike watched as the browser brought up a website.

A warm glowing sun shone in a blue sky, thin clouds softening the edges. Its rays stretched out like arms in a benediction. The sun sank slowly behind rolling hills, its final gleam illuminating a blue stone stela that marked the rise of a spring.

The picture sharpened its focus on the spring. Markings on the stela had been weathered away to simply an impression. Now a halo'd moon rose in the sharp night.

Mike frowned. Had he seen that image before?

'What we do is write out a curse tablet,' said Thorby.

Mike returned his attention to the man. 'Pardon?'

'I said that you write out a *curse tablet* and then use your credit card to pay for a silver coin to *toss* into the stream. And the spirit of the stream will answer your prayer. But I didn't know it was real,' Thorby said. 'I didn't know. It was just another executive toy--you know like voodoo dolls or those foam bricks to throw at the fucking computer when it goes wrong again. That's all it was.'

'That spring's the one where they found the girl's body,' said Kilbride.

Mike glanced at Thorby. 'That's where I saw it, on the telly.'

'I didn't know anything about it until the police came banging on the door,' Thorby said. 'She was my ex-girl friend--a right bitch.' Then he bent over biting his knuckle. 'It must be a coincidence.'

'I've lost all belief in coincidence,' Mike said. 'OK, I suppose you wrote out a curse tablet. Very Roman. What did you put on it?'

Thorby's breath was shaky. He grabbed a fresh tissue from a box labeled *man-sized, extra-absorbent*. His fiddling hands ripped it into pieces as he spoke. 'I wrote *I hate her, I wish she were dead*. But I didn't mean it. It was like an anger management exercise. You write a grumble down and put it in the grumble jar and then open the jar next week and see if anything is still valid. It makes you feel better to write things like that down, get them out. I didn't kill her. Oh God! Why did I write it?'

Mike couldn't stop himself. 'If we all cursed our exes there'd be no women left in the world.' It had been years since he'd thought about Sally.

He turned away from the weeping man and touched his hands to the screen. Trying to clear his mind, he thought of the sea. Rolling waves coming in on the tide. White horses dancing on the crest of each breaker. And slowly she was banished from his thoughts.

'What's he doing?' asked Thorby, but his voice was distant now.

'Hush,' whispered Kilbride.

Mike felt his eyelids droop as he watched the spring and the stela. His mind flowed with the water. It sank underground. The Romans had built an aqueduct; he could see the stone tiles, and then the lead lining.

It surged upwards, joyously breaking free of the earth and spraying into the bright sky.

Mike took his hands from the screen and walked blindly across the room.

'Stop him!' shouted Thorby. 'He's going out the window.'

Mike felt hands on his arms, he opened his eyes and looked down three stories into a courtyard. A fountain welled up in freshly sandblasted Victorian marble.

The water turned to blood.

The taint of hot metallic mess stung his throat.

'It's poison,' he whispered. He could feel the darkness clawing at his heart. It pushed on his lungs making him gulp for air.

'What the hell's going on?' Thorby demanded. 'Is he a psychic thingy? I saw that in a police drama on the telly.'

'Shut up!'

Mike felt hands grip his elbows.

They dragged him away from the window.

Blood dripped down the walls.

They forced him into a chair.

A stinging slap over his face rocked his head back.

'Mike!'

Skeletons crept out from where they had been swept under the carpet.

His face stung again.

'Mike!'

Mike blinked. He squinted as the corporate white paint spun around, blinding him.

'Here Mike, drink this.' Kilbride offered a bottle of Lucozade.

With a shaking hand Mike clutched the bottle and glugged the liquid as if it were aqua vitae. The room stabilized.

'What was here?'

'This whole building is covered in death,' Mike said. 'The spring is linked to the fountain down there. But the link is stronger than that. We need to get down there.'

He jumped to his feet and the walls wavered slightly. He grabbed the desk, and swigged the Lucozade. Gasping a little, he staggered to the door.

'What's with him?'

Mike looked back into the room. 'Get up and come with us, now.'

Kilbride quietly hitched a hand through Thorby's elbow. 'I could get nasty if you decide to struggle.'

Thorby threw his scraps of tissue on the table and snatched a handful from the box.

Satisfied they were following, Mike kept a hand on the wall as he walked to the lifts. While they descended in silence, the glucose drink warmed him. By the time the doors opened, the universe had stabilized.

Mike peered out and saw Anita Glade carrying a parcel out of the main entrance. He ducked back, and held out a hand to stop the others from exiting. He checked the lobby again. Once she was out of sight, he turned to the others.

'What's the nearest exit to the fountain court?' Mike asked.

Thorby nodded a direction. 'That one.' His face was pale.

A security guard looked in their direction, then levered himself to his feet. He walked across as they reached the outer door.

'What's happening here?'

Mike stopped and smiled. 'We're actors,' he said. 'We've got lapel cams, it's gonna be like the Blair Witch Project film you know? It's all permitted, of course.'

The guard's face went blank.

'Oh! Yes,' continued Mike. 'Our special FX's team will be playing some neat tricks on that Fountain. So don't worry if you see anything odd.'

'OK. I'll get back to work,' said the guard.

'I'll have to remember that one,' said Kilbride.

'I find it easier to work with an easily recognizable cultural reference.'

'What are you two talking about? What did you do to that man?' Thorby stared at the guard, who had sat back down at his station and was stuffing crisps in his maw while staring at the CCTV screens.

Mike shrugged. 'It's like *the Force*. Let's go.'

Pushing open a wired fire-glass door into the courtyard, Mike thought he caught a taint of blood on the wind. He took a deep breath and strode across the cobbles to the marble. A soppy little cupid vomited water from its mouth and shot its arrow at anyone entering the yard through the main archway to the road. Some clever design by the architect muted the noise from the road. Four topiary trees lived a constricted life in faux-lead planters; the rest of the square courtyard was paved.

Mike ran a hand down the topiary spiral, but felt nothing amiss. Reluctantly he walked over to the fountain and put hands on the basin. Shimmering under the water were hundreds of silver coins.

Suddenly the cherub was a skeleton, dripping carved marble worms.

'*Help us! Justice! I hate him, kill him! I know he's the one who dug up my plants, I hope that horrid little terrier is run over. Help us!*'

Mike slammed his hands over his ears, but the voices of the curse tablets sang their cruel songs into his head.

'Mike! I shouldn't have called someone with such clear vision!'

'It's OK,' Mike said. He ran a hand through his light brown hair. 'I'll be OK.'

'So this is the center of the business? The murderer for hire is here in this building?'

'I'm sure of it.'

'Fine,' said Kilbride. He reached up and tweaked a hair from Thorby's head, yanking it out by the root.

'Hey!' Thorby clapped his free hand to his head. 'What'd you do that for?'

Kilbride examined the hair and nodded. 'Mike, could you sit over there with Thorby while I do a few summonings?'

Mike dropped a hand onto the hapless programmer's shoulder. 'Come with me.'

'Why do I have to stay? I need to get back to work,' said Thorby.

'What makes you think you'll *ever* go back to work?' Mike led the man to a marble bench that stood on the edge of the little courtyard. 'You've got to pay for hiring someone to kill your ex-girlfriend.'

'But I didn't. It wasn't me. I...'

'You should watch this,' Mike said. 'Curse tablets aren't the only thing that the Romans brought to Britannia.'

Still holding the hair, Kilbride produced a flask from his pocket.

Mike wondered what alcohol Kilbride carried in his flask.

Kilbride drew a thin circle around the fountain, then he stood just outside the line, his hands open in supplication, Thorby's hair balanced over his left palm.

Mike barely felt the prickly-heat sensation of strength directed towards fire summoning.

Thorby wriggled and loosened his collar and tie.

A beautiful woman, all shimmery and silver, like a fish, rose from the water. Her dress flashed in the sunlight like a waterfall.

Mike resisted a snicker as Thorby's mouth dropped open. This was no laughing matter.

'It's a naiad,' Mike said. 'They guard sacred springs and they are required to answer Curse Tablets.'

'But... but ... it's not real.'

Mike shrugged. 'OK, you're suffering a hallucination from the stress of the past few days.'

'Why have you called me, nature hater?' The naiad's voice sang like summer rain after a long drought.

'I have called you here to account for the death of humans,' answered Kilbride.

The silver woman cowered. 'But I do what I am impelled to do, sweet master. Don't send me into the fire-death, please sweet master.'

'Who acts as your interface with the substantial world?'

'Sweet master, I needed worshipers. They have forgotten the supplications and invocations. I starve.'

Wringing her hands, she leant towards Kilbride.

He let her.

Her watery body lengthened until the circle flared up between them.

'Arrrrrrgh! Master!' she screamed. Steam rose into the air and her body mass shrank.

Thorby grabbed at Mike's arm. 'Stop him! He's killing her.'

The naiad sank into the fountain pond.

'They always try that, you know,' Mike said conversationally. 'If she gets her tongue down your throat you're a gonner.'

'How can you be so casual about... things like that being... alive?'

'Because we serve seven years apprenticeship,' Mike said.

Thorby watched, horrified as Kilbride dragged her out of the pond into her human-like form.

'Summon your interface, if you please,' said Kilbride.

The naiad's gaze traveled around the courtyard and stopped on Thorby. She pointed and shrieked, 'Ask him. Ask the supplicant. He dealt with her.'

'I swear I only used the web interface. I never met a human.'

'Summon your Priestess,' ordered Kilbride. 'Thrice I have asked. Do I have to command you.'

The creature cowered back against the cherub, hiding her face in her watery hair.

The topiary tree nearest the archway was fading into mist. Mike glanced at the sky. It was still only mid-afternoon. He looked back and saw fog creeping through the archway. He could just about make out a figure lurking in the shadows.

Kilbride stayed focused on the naiad, his fire wards crawling towards the fountain.

The fog reached out tentacles that wrapped around the faux-lead planter nearest Kilbride.

Abruptly, the topiary tree reached out and smacked him upside the head.

Kilbride staggered at the attack.

He fell to the paving slabs but rolled and was back on his feet, facing the entryway. With the loss of his concentration, the wards fizzled out.

The naiad spurted up in a fountain of rage.

Kilbride cast his hand towards the tree and shouted, '*He shall rain fire and brimstone upon them.*'

The tree burst into flames and Kilbride rolled out of the way of the pouncing naiad.

As it fell towards the burning topiary, it spread out, like a cloak of water.

Mike jumped to his feet. 'I'd better join in. Stay there, hey?' He judged where he was needed, and added, 'This mist might be a bit toxic, so try not to breath too much.'

Thorby tried to leap off the bench and his face fell as he found he was glued to the stone.

'Ah! That did work, good! Only joking about the mist.'

Mike appraised the situation--Kilbride was fully occupied with the naiad. He kicked the burning tree from the path of the descending water. Slipping his hand into his pocket, he brought out his flask again. Jumping over the flooding on the pavement, that was trying to pull him flat and drown him, he tossed some of the liquid from his flask on the burning tree.

It flared up, and then Kilbride back-kicked the tree, sending it into the middle of the flood.

Steam hissed up, joining the fog lining the courtyard.

Mike pulled the mist around him. Thorby was trying to peer through the fog, which now had softened the edges of the courtyard. He held a tissue over his mouth and nose.

Mike sniggered. Obviously the man took his warning about the mist seriously.

As Mike drifted with the fog towards the archway, he made out a dim figure.

A voice shouted, '*He lets us see clearly when evil clouds our sight.*'

Hastily, Mike pulled the glass and concrete walls around him like a familiar coat. The acrid stench of burning tree and the heat of the steam all covered him in their friendly camouflage.

The mist cleared.

'Anita! What are you doing here?' Kilbride peered around his sister.

Mike moved as slowly as mountains, as slowly as rock.

'As always, you are blind to what you don't want to see,' said Anita. 'I'm here to stop you from destroying my second income.'

She gestured and watery hands caught hold of Kilbride's feet.

'Anita?'

'I know you won't raise a hand against your sister.' Anita laughed. 'You are such a gentleman.'

Kilbride looked sad. 'You're right, I won't harm you. But I'm not alone, you see. Mike Rider, I hand control of this investigation to you.'

Kilbride turned away from his sister. 'I call on the sun to bind this creature.'

'What? Where?' Anita spun around looking for Mike. 'He's not here, you fool. You've let your mind get as old as your body. You could choose to do neither, if you had the courage, and now you're going to drown! Drown!'

She raised her hands above her head and the water surged over his ankles and up to his knees.

Mike moved with pace of a solid wall.

Kilbride struggled for all the heat workings he could without drowning himself. The water oozed up to waist-height. Kilbride lowered his arms and waited.

With the speed of an avalanche, Mike ran across the remaining courtyard.

'*He summons lightning to his hands.*' Mike spread his hands and lightning flew from the fingertips. '*In lightning he cages the evil-doer.*'

As if hitting a Faraday cage, the lightning spread out into bars.

Anita reached out a hand. Fog began to swirl around her again. As it hit the bars of the cage, the electricity conducted into her hand, and through her whole body. A hideous smell of burnt hair filled the courtyard.

Anita collapsed to the pavement.

Mike spun on his heel. Kilbride had his chin lifted as he fought to keep his mouth and nose free of the rising tide.

Mike sprinted across the courtyard. He ripped the tissue off Thorby and shook it out. Holding it out at arm's length he shouted,

'*And the sea was parted as if it was sucked dry.*'

He held the tissue against the naiad. A hideous squeal sounded--like a drowning pig.

The naiad pulled back against the absorbency of the tissue. 'Master let me live! I do what I am instructed.'

Kilbride's hands were free now. He gripped the bottom corners of the tissue, delicately. The soggy tissue could tear.

'*The sun and winds will dry up the ocean.*' Kilbride added his strength to Mike's and the naiad was sucked into cotton softness.

'*He burneth the chariots of war.*'

Held between them, the tissue twisted as it struggled to be free. Steam rose from the tissue, then from the center it burst into flames. The two men held onto their corners until they were in danger of being burnt. Every part of the tissue burnt to ash before drifting to the paving slabs.

'*Thou shalt break the ships of the sea with the East wind.*'

A gust rushed through the archway. It picked up the fragments of ash and carried them high above the company building.

'No!' Anita screamed from the archway.

Mike looked over. His cage had died, but Anita sat in a puddle staring at her hands. Her shiny hair became staring with lank strands of gray. Wrinkles ran over her face like rivers carving gorges.

Weeping wildly, she buried her face in hands that blossomed age spots.

Kilbride smiled grimly. 'I forgot to mention that Anita is my eldest sister. I thought it was botox and dye, I swear.'

'I gathered the seniority, from the family dynamics. My sister is older than me. I'll take her in, shall I?'

Kilbride nodded. He turned away from the rocking scarecrow that had been a bright executive. 'I'll take the young man.'

'He's glued to that bench. Sorry, I was in a hurry.'

Kilbride strode away.

Mike levered Anita to her feet. He walked her through the lobby past the security guard.

The guard looked up from his screens. Mike suddenly realized the whole fight was recorded on CCTV.

'Them special FX's were fab. Can't wait until the movie comes out,' the guard said.

He Dreams of Justice

Detective Inspector Gargate pushed open the heavy oak doors of the church and peered inside. These old churches were built like castles, complete with a huge beam across the door to bar the unworthy from entry.

At the altar, a young man in a dog collar stood trimming the candles. Gargate fumbled with the card in his pocket. Then he walked up to the vicar.

Hearing the footsteps on the stone flags, the vicar turned with an easy smile. 'Can I help you?'

Gargate held out the card. 'I need to contact... umm.'

The vicar looked at the card then up at Gargate. For a moment Gargate was sure he was onto something, but the vicar's face became a mask of puzzlement.

'I'm sorry, I don't quite know what you mean. If you need to contact God, you've come to the right place.' The vicar smiled hopefully.

Gargate sagged. 'Sorry, I thought you'd know, what with the cross on the card.' He looked down at the oblong of white card on his hand, simply printed with a red cross.

'It doesn't look like a calling card I'd use. Sorry.'

Gargate left the vicar to his candles and pushed out through the oak doors. He had been so sure that he had the answer to these cards.

The paving slabs were uneven on the path leading away from the church. If they didn't watch out, they would end up getting sued when some tourist tripped over the uneven flags.

He walked slowly towards the lychgate, which marked the transition between sacred and secular ground.

He stopped with his hand on the gate's latch. Hold on a moment, how had the vicar known it was a calling card?

As he turned, he heard the bar being pushed across the inside of the door. He sagged. Apparently, as a secular authority, he was unworthy here.

In his pocket, he crushed the card in his fist. His last hope, gone. He drove back to the station and made his way to his office.

Opening the door, he found the room had been stripped of his computer and files.

'Mr. Gargate,' said his secretary, her lip curling in disgust. 'You are wanted in the Chief Inspector's office immediately.' She retreated from him as fast as humanly possible.

He looked after her in considerable alarm. Why would his secretary act like that?

He shrugged. The answer would be in the Chief's office.

As he walked along, people he had worked with scuttled of his way, almost as if he were carrying an infectious disease.

Pretending not to notice, he tapped on the Chief's door and entered.

The Chief sat behind his desk and didn't rise as his Inspector entered. There was another senior officer present, standing beside the chief.

'There you are Dan,' said the Chief. 'Acting on information received, we have been forced to impound your computer. And a very brief survey of the contents of your inbox have lead us to believe that you are not suitable to work in the Force.'

'What?' spluttered Gargate. 'There's nothing on my computer, either here or at home that could merit suspension. What is this information? Who gave it to you?'

'The forensic boys have found your stash of child pornography,' said the Chief.

'What? There's nothing like that on my computer.'

'They tell me you didn't even password protect the file,' said the Chief, sadly. 'I thought you were one of my clean lads, Dan.'

'But...'

'Inspector Harris will escort you from the building. You may collect your personal effects from your former office. Con will check that you take nothing belonging to the department with you. Your mail, if it is personal, will be forwarded to your house.'

'Who has planted this stuff on me?' demanded Gargate. 'I've never looked at that...'

The Chief looked at him, sadly. 'Your wife found distressing images on your home computer and contacted us.'

'Liza! She wouldn't! There isn't anything like that on my home computer--just like there was nothing on there this morning before I...'

Gargate remembered the barred church. He sagged.

'Before what?'

'Nothing,' said Gargate. What had he done? What had he set off when he showed that card to the vicar?

He stormed out of the Chief's office, followed by Harris. He had to get home to Liza. Surely she'd believe that the pictures were planted. They'd been married ten years.

'Don't know why you're denying it,' said Harris. 'Those pictures were found on your computer.'

Gargate stopped his headlong charge. Grabbing Harris by the shirt he put his face into Harris's. 'Someone has planted that junk on me and you know it, if you know me at all. We trained together, Con. How could *you* believe I would have anything to do with... with...'

He pushed Harris away and resumed his stride. He had to get home.

Again, people ducked out of meeting his eyes.

How could anyone believe this charge? He had worked with them for years.

Once he was outside the building, it was worse. Someone had alerted the press.

Cameras flashed in his eyes as the doors slid open. He tried to step backwards, to retreat from the attack of lights, but Harris stood barring his way, a smug smile on his lips.

Forced out, he pushed aside the cameramen and ran to his car, his only thought to get home and talk to Liza. She *had* to understand.

He had his keys out and was in his car, but the press barred his path out. He had to endure a slow millimeter drive out of the staff carpark with the flashing lights blinding him.

When he arrived home he wasn't sure how he'd got there. Here too, the press were hanging around the drive, but he pressed the button on his remote and drove straight into the garage. With the door as a barrier between the world and his haven, he leaned against the steering wheel.

After a few deep breaths, he squeezed out of the car. He only normally parked his car in here on weekends and it was full of junk.

He let himself into the house and knew immediately the house was empty. There was a note on the kitchen table. He left it there.

He went into the study. She had left his computer turned on. With the mouse, he flicked through page after page of images that turned his stomach.

Driven from his sanctum, he ran to their bedroom. His clothes had been flung about, his pajamas were ripped apart.

He checked in Joe's room, then Ellie's. Here too he found evidence of rapid packing. She had gone, and taken the children with her.

He slid down the wall at the top of the stairs and sat with his hands clasped between his knees.

She had believed that he would download those disgusting images.

She had gone.

How long he sat there he had no idea. It was getting dark when he heard a noise downstairs: a key scraping in the lock.

Hope lit up his life. 'Liza?' He scrambled to his feet. 'Liza?'

He took the stairs in two bounds and staggered into the kitchen and flicked on the light. Three young men, dressed in jeans and shirts under long raincoats stood in his kitchen. The light didn't surprise them. One had his arm locked behind him, before he could draw in the breath to demand their business.

'The Council doesn't like people prying,' whispered the man behind him.

'Wait a minute, I wasn't...'

Another of the men punched him in the stomach. He bent over the pain, the wind knocked out of him. Then the men dragged him out of the house.

The press had gone but a van stood on the drive. They had ropes ready in the van. Two of the men pushed him in.

Still winded, he tried to kick out, but one of them grabbed his foot and twisted until he screamed. The third man in the group stood outside the van, holding a stick just above the ground.

Not one of the curtains in house next door even twitched.

These men weren't street fighters, they were properly trained.

A few twists of rope and he was trussed like a Christmas turkey.

'Wait,' he gasped. 'I just wanted...'

The leader put his face to Gargate's. He could smell the curry on the man's breath.

'Shut up.' The leader slapped duck tape over Gargate's mouth and climbed out of the van.

'Did you have to be so rough?' asked the man who waited outside.

'You know what the Council said.'

'There are easier ways to do it.'

'Only for you, Karl.'

'Coming as I do from a family, many of whom qualified under the Council,' said the man who had punched him. 'I say with surety, that this is the traditional way of dealing with this sort of problem.'

The leader rolled his eyes as he slammed the rear door. Then the three of them climbed in the front of the van and started the engine. It pulled slowly out of the drive.

It made a kind of sense that they would drive with due care for the rules of the road, they wouldn't want to be stopped with a captive in the rear. Though he felt from the way his former colleagues had reacted, that they would happily join this group in whatever they had planned.

But there was dissension in the ranks. If he got his mouth free, could he appeal to Karl?

The journey wasn't a long one, which meant he was still in London. The van pulled to a halt and then the engine switched off.

'Karl, keep the wards over us. Jerry help me with him.'

As he was dragged out, Gargate noticed that Karl held his stick between them and the road. The faded orange lights from the street let him see Karl's look of extreme concentration about him, a look that collapsed once they had him inside a building--a warehouse from the look of it.

With his feet tied, he couldn't walk.

The two men each shoved a hand under his arm and dragged him through a breeze block corridor.

Karl shuffled past them and pushed open a door. He cast a worried look at Gargate and Gargate tried to beg for help with his eyes.

Jerry and the leader dropped him face up on the concrete floor. Gargate tried to look around but could only move his eyes.

Bare light bulbs cast sharp light over the scene. There were about ten more men in the room ranging from late teens to mid twenties. It looked like Karl and the leader were the oldest men here.

But Karl stayed by the door watching the group.

'Now what do we do?' one of the men asked the leader.

'The Council said to make sure no missed him,' said the leader.

'We've done that,' interrupted Jerry. 'Just like my Uncle told me they used to do. It's a lot easier with computers. No one will miss the nasty pedophile. Even his wife left him.

The leader frowned at Jerry. 'And get him admitted to the treatment center, preferably by hospital.'

'So we have to send a madman walking the streets?' asked a red-haired teen. 'That doesn't sound right.'

'I'm sure you find it frustrating when the Council orders actions you don't understand' Jerry said. 'But a first year shouldn't question his instructions. You're not from a family that has had a member of this college for six generations. This is how it has always been dealt with. We should get started.'

Redhead looked at Karl, who shifted his gaze away.

'Yes,' said the leader. 'Let's get this over with.'

Gargate felt tension building, like a thunderstorm. It started as a headache at the base of his skull.

'Allow me to show you how. *My bones are smitten asunder, as with a sword,*' shouted Jerry. He smiled in satisfaction.

If Gargate's mouth had been free, he would have screamed. It felt like millstones were grinding his leg bones. A muffled grunt escaped around the tape over his mouth.

'*I thirsted and they gave me vinegar to drink.*'

His throat was raw and burning. He wanted to cry out, *No! I only wanted Justice*, but the words in his mind were lost in the pain.

Things crawled all over him. Cramps dug into his stomach and his body rebelled. The room swayed with what ever it was they were doing.

'Stop it!' shouted Redhead. 'This is wrong!'

The tension in the room vanished. Tears of relief leaked down his face, and blocked his sight. He could barely breathe through the snot in his nose and snorted it back down his throat into his offended stomach. He swallowed hard, knowing he couldn't vomit against the tape.

There was a scuffled and a thump of a body falling to the ground.

Squinting as the bright bulb blinded him, Gargate saw Jerry lifting a hand to thump a prone Redhead.

Then Karl thwacked Jerry's raised arm with his staff.

'No! We don't turn on our own. Especially not first years. Out of the mouths of innocence,' Karl said. 'He's right and you know it.'

'Karl,' said the leader, patiently. 'We can't question the Council's ruling.'

Redhead sprang to his feet and stood next to Karl. His mouth was bleeding. 'If there weren't people brave enough to question the rulers then nothing wrong would ever be changed.'

Karl frowned at Redhead. 'I'm just saying that whatever the Council says, we don't fight among ourselves.'

Jerry fisted his hands. 'With our responsibilities, we cannot make these sorts of decisions ourselves. Years of precedent argue in favor of this method.'

The leader spread his hands between Karl and Jerry. 'Karl, could you and Josh please withdraw. We will follow the Council's orders.'

Gargate writhed, trying to attract attention.

Karl looked down. Hurriedly, he crouched and ripped off the tape.

Relieved, Gargate vomited over the floor.

Karl danced back, keeping his boots free of the mess.

'Stupid thing to do,' yelled Karl. 'You can kill people like that.' He grabbed Red-haired Josh and walked to one side.

Josh tried to get back, but Karl spoke quietly in his ear.

A hand gripped Gargate's hair and pulled him away from the puddle of vomit. The leader stared at Karl then down at Gargate. The group of men passed looks between Karl and Jerry.

'Help me!' Gargate tried to shout, but his plea barely passed his lips. If only he could pass out, but the harsh lights of the room drowned out the shades of gray.

'Help me,' he whispered towards Karl.

While holding a restraining hand on Josh's shoulder, Karl produced a mobile from his coat pocket. He straightened, almost at attention, as he began speaking.

Gargate could feel the tension rising again. 'No! No!' he whispered, but there was no one listening.

He lost track of time as creatures crawled over him and bit him. He closed his eyes and tried to find some darkness to hide in, but the light from the bare bulbs clung to him. Then monstrous shadows poured in from the corners of the room, threatening to eat him. He struggled to sit only to find that odd pressure pushing him down. Fire burned his feet and hand and crawled up his arms and legs. He screamed but couldn't hear a sound.

He heard running footsteps.

'See nothing happens to him, he says,' grumbled Karl. 'Here, hold my staff and prevent physical attack.'

Then the tension stopped. It felt as if a spring rain was falling joyfully on the garden. The feeling was so strong that he opened his eyes, expecting to be standing at his open kitchen door.

Karl stood astride him, his arms spread wide. Next to him, Josh stood nervously, holding the staff. The others were standing looking grim-faced, and he sensed that Karl was holding off the creepy crawlies.

The six younger members of the group slid backwards and stood in a circle around the group. Karl faced down Jerry and the leader.

'This is not correct behavior,' Jerry said. 'What makes you so righteous to decide to go against the rules?'

Karl shook his head. The curious expression of concentration was back on his face. The calm wavered. Gargate felt waves of anger from the others who had been shown up as wrong.

Gargate wriggled closer to his protector and curled up around the man's ankles.

Then the door slammed open. The odd sensations vanished immediately.

'Just what is going on here?' demanded a new voice.

Gargate managed to open his eyes a crack and saw an older man stalk into the room.

Karl stepped away and then sagged. The staff clattered to the floor as Josh grabbed Karl and helped him sit.

All the men looked between the new man and the leader.

'The Council ordered us to do it, Mr. Dunkley.' The leader cast a look of loathing at where Karl and Josh crouched near Gargate.

Dunkley strode across the room. He dug a hand in his pocket and pulled out a handgun. He pressed this into the leader's hand.

'Kill him,' Dunkley said.

The leader looked at the gun in his hand. His gaze flicking between Dunkley and Gargate. 'But...'

'I tell you to kill him.' Dunkley folded his arms.

Gargate whispered, 'No! Please no!'

The leader turned with the gun in his hand and slipped the safety off. Gargate tried to wriggle away, but there was nowhere to hide in this bare room.

'Sir!' shouted Josh.

Dunkley held up a hand silencing the youth, but remained watching the leader.

The leader lowered the gun. 'I can't kill in cold blood, sir! What has he done?'

Dunkley retrieved his weapon, put on the safety and pocketed it. 'Precisely, Mr. Meredith, what *has* he done? Shall we ask him?'

Gargate heard footsteps walking over to him. Sobbing with relief at still being alive, he tried to sit, but the ropes kept him prone.

A cold knife slid down his wrists, and then along his ankles. The ropes fell away and firm hands helped him straighten.

He sat, looking blearily at his rescuer who was much older than his captors. This Dunkley wore a suit. Gargate focused on the man's top button, undone, with the tie loosened, as if he had just started to relax for the evening before this call for help.

The others group into two camps: Karl and Josh crouched nearby, the others looking like they wished they were elsewhere.

He suddenly noticed he was filthy.

Dunkley knelt on one knee next to him. 'So what did you do to annoy the Council?'

'I don't even know what Council you're talking about,' he croaked.

Dunkley rest two fingers on his throat. '*And he brought waters to soothe our parched throats.*'

The pain was gone. He could speak.

'Thank you.'

'Tell me what happened today,' Dunkley said.

'I went to ask a vicar to help me contact...' He fumbled in his pocket with numb fingers. He managed to clutch the screwed-up business card and offered it to Dunkley.

Dunkley accepted the crumpled ball and flattened it in his fingers. 'Ah!' he said.

'Then the day just went wrong. Someone set me up as a pedophile.'

He couldn't stop the catch in his voice.

Dunkley put a reassuring hand on his shoulder. 'You're unlucky. Normally these calls are routed to me, but I was out of town--on business. Why did you want to see us?'

'There's a man--the coroner has declared it suicide, but there were a lot of things about the case that suggested if it were followed up it would lead to one of those cards. I found a message on his computer, "Your Ancestors are waiting for you..." His wife swore he had no reason to kill himself. We're told early in our careers never to ask questions about these cards. They represent a dream of Justice where none would be permitted in the waking world. But I only wanted Justice for a young father. That's all.'

Without looking up Dunkley said, 'I think you gentlemen need to return to your Halls.'

Jerry stood his ground. 'This isn't how things used to be done. My Uncle is right. We've gone soft, from the top down. We...'

'Have no Christian compassion? Is that it, Mr. Wyndlyffe?' Dunkley stayed on his knee beside Gargate as he looked up at Jerry. 'I remember your Uncle--he was one of my tutors. So he told you all about the old days did he? Did he mention the time when I was in my second year and I wiped the gym floor with his face?'

Jerry face turned purple.

'Perhaps you can right a wrong,' Dunkley said. 'I'll see you in the gym at nine tomorrow, perhaps your skills can persuade me where your words cannot.'

Jerry spun on his heel. The high color drained from his face as he stormed out of the warehouse. The others shuffled out as Josh helped Karl to his feet.

'Karl, thank you. Mr. Analay, please ensure Mr. Stempress eats soonest.'

'Yes, sir!' Josh said.

When all of them were gone. Dunkley help Gargate to his feet. Then with an arm under his shoulder he half carried Gargate to a car. The van had gone.

'I'm a mess,' protested Gargate, exhausted by the walk out to the car. He wanted to collapse in a heap.

'There's been worse in this car,' Dunkley said. He strapped Gargate into the seat.

Gargate rested his head back against the headrest and tried not to cry. He felt the engine start and the car pulled gently away.

'Why?' he asked, without opening his eyes.

The indicator clicked rhythmically. 'Until a few years ago this was standard practice. It was considered a way of toughening up the gentlemen. The Council is made up of men who believe in traditions. I had to go through it, and swore I would see it didn't happen again. I'm sorry.'

'How did they...?' he stopped and opened his eyes. 'Was that... magic?'

He saw Dunkley smile ruefully. 'We don't use magic. I find the distinction quite important. Unfortunately, some of our people use their strength as if it were magic.'

Dunkley pulled up at his drive and came to the passenger side to help him out. 'I will investigate your case and report back to you.'

Dunkley had driven away, before Gargate remembered that he had never once given his address. He stumbled up the drive and through the garage. Thankfully the door was unlocked. He staggered into the kitchen and to the cupboard where the cooking sherry was kept.

The bottle rattled on the tumbler, then he drained it in one long swallow. He was about to pour another one.

Then he saw her sitting at the table. She had lifted her head as if she had just woken up and her mouth dropped open in horror.

'Oh Dan! What have they done to you?'

'Liza! I...' He left the bottle and sank into a chair at the table. Relief that she was here. He couldn't stop the tears. Liza crouched at his side and held him.

'I got to my mother's and she said, "I don't believe that of Dan!" and suddenly I knew that you wouldn't. That it was a set up and I had told your boss. Oh Dan, I'm sorry, I...'

Gargate pulled her close and stared into her eyes. 'I wouldn't download that stuff, ever.'

'I know. I left the kids with mother and came back. I've been waiting for you.' She sniffed delicately. 'You stink, let's get you in the shower.'

* * * *

A week later, Gargate sat answering the letter from his solicitor about claiming compensation for wrongful suspension when he found another envelope on his desk.

The postmark was smudged. Curious, he slit it open. A simple card, printed only with a red cross, fell onto his desk.

He was satisfied.

Some Fall by Virtue

'Does he know where we're going?' Chirstie asked. 'As I said, we should have brought a map.'

Trewithick sighed and muttered, 'For the fifteenth time.'

'What was that?' Chirstie paused for a moment with her foot on a rock. Even in this drizzle she looked flustered by the hill walk. The hood on her coat made her look even more like a plastic doll than she had last night. At least all her make-up was drip proof, now they were up among the low clouds that covered the hills her face would have melted.

Trewithick smiled slightly as he paused to stay with her. 'Only that we're still on Dunkley's own land. He scampered all over these hills as a boy.'

She frowned at that, then shrugged. 'We should be going back. It was bad enough with all that drizzle, but now it's getting foggy. This is not weather for walking.'

Trewithick sighed. 'It's closer to walk on than return from here. And.' He smiled, trying to reassure her. 'If we go on we'll be above the clouds shortly. That is the reason we came on this hike away from the warm fireplaces of the lodge.'

Loose pebbles skittered down the path.

Chirstie shrank behind Trewithick as a huge black shape shambled out of the mist.

Trewithick cast a scornful glance at Chirstie. 'Here, boy!'

The huge wolfhound trotted over to Trewithick and accepted an ear rub. Trewithick checked the collar.

'It's only Rory,' he said.

'God! It looks fierce.'

More pebbles fell down the path, heralding Dunkley scrambling down hill, emerging from the mist.

Ross, the second hound, walked at Dunkley's side. One or two stones bounced far enough to land in the scree slope below. They heard the rattling, like peas in a child's shaker, which reminded them there was a long, currently unseen, drop from the path.

Like Trewithick, Dunkley wore a hat to protect his face from the rain, rather than his coat hood.

'What's the trouble?' Dunkley asked.

Trewithick opened his mouth to offer an easy excuse, but Chirstie jumped in with a warning glance at him.

'I've just got a stone in my shoe,' she said.

Trewithick raised an eyebrow, but said nothing.

Dunkley rolled his eyes. 'Look, Nathaniel, I need to get back to the rest of the group before they get bored and start on the down path without me. It's a bit tricky in these low clouds and I don't want those unfamiliar with this area leaving the path. But you know the way--show Miss Leaker, will you?'

Only Dunkley saw the grimace as Trewithick said, 'Of course, see you at the pub.'

'You've got your phone on you?'

Trewithick nodded.

'Call if you get too late.' Dunkley grinned at his friend and scrambled back up the path, his waist length plait disappearing into the mist.

'God! He's fit isn't he? Unless he's putting on a show for the tourists.'

Trewithick chose not to reply. 'Would you like to rest a while, since the rest of the group won't be waiting for us?'

'What? Where would I sit in this horrible weather?' said Chirstie. 'Let's just keep going.'

Trewithick set foot on the up path again but Chirstie pushed past him, trying to gain some speed. Her waterproof trousers hushing as counterpoint to the rain tapping on his hat.

Trewithick followed her easily.

If I closed my eyes, he thought, *I could follow the sound of her voice.*

He wondered if she ever stopped talking. Perhaps he should try plugging her mouth, but the only thing he had to hand was kisses. He suddenly grinned; from her admiration of Dunkley, he suspected he'd get slapped if he tried it.

She was now going on about rainfall levels dropping in the southern counties. He interrupted her monologue.

'See the cloud is getting lighter now.'

'No you're mistaken,' she said. 'The drizzle is as persistent as ever.'

'Brighter, I meant. The light is shining through the clouds,' he said. 'We're getting close to the top.'

She looked around, but couldn't deny the fact that it was brighter. 'Well, it will be good to get out of the rain. Do you think they will have waited for us? I would have waited if one of my party had needed to stop to clear a shoe.'

Trewithick smiled slightly. Chirstie had managed to annoy everyone this weekend. He doubted anyone would wait for her--and to that regard, him. Sometimes he wished his mother had been less insistent on good manners. Unconsciously, he rubbed the back of his hand.

They burst through the last clouds. The demarcation was so abrupt it took a moment for his glasses to catch up and turn dark.

He rubbed his eyes and wiped the damp from his face, then turned to see what Chirstie made of the cloud inversion.

All around them was white; the tops of the hills showed thorough like islands in a cloudy sea that filled the valleys. The white was blinding, if one didn't happen to be wearing reactolight lenses and a wide-brimmed hat.

Chirstie shaded her eyes with her hand and pushed back the hood of her waterproof. In the bright sunlight up here, it even felt warm after the strenuous climb. She unzipped the waterproof, exposing her sky blue sweater and the collar of her blouse embroidered with yellow flowers.

'We can rest for a while up here,' he said, smiling. 'These stones will be dry.'

'I can't see them waiting,' she said.

'They'll be in the pub when we get there.' They'd better be.

Trewithick perched on a rock, so that she'd get the hint and try and have a rest. The slow pace on the way up here had tried his patience.

'Oh are you tired,' she said. 'I did wonder.' She flopped onto the rock beside him. 'How come you know Alasdair Dunkley?'

Trewithick sighed. 'We went to the same school.'

'But you're quite a bit older than him.'

'Seven years,' he said, smiling at memory. 'Chosen first years got to wait on the Prefects' studies. I chose Dunkley.'

'You and he are...were...' Her face was a picture.

Trewithick snorted with laughter. 'There seems to be an odd impression, in people who don't attend public school, as to what happens there. He made my toast and polished my shoes.'

'I've been wanting to ask, why isn't he Laird Dunkley? People all say he is head of the clan.'

'His father is still alive,' Trewithick said. He got to his feet and turned away from her. 'I think it's time we headed down.'

'But why...?'

Trewithick only managed a cold smile. 'If you want to know about Laird Dunkley, ask someone else--not me, not Alasdair. Will you come on?' He set out at his normal pace.

'But I was just wanting to know,' she said. 'It's not like I can ask him. Sorry if I offended you, but you have to see that as his closest friend you're the obvious person to ask. You need to slow down, you might get worn out again.'

Trewithick glanced down at her. She was puffing already, but he wasn't prepared to slow down yet. 'This is my usual pace. I would like to be at the pub before dark.'

The path led along a ridge and down towards the clouds. The sun behind them cast their shadows on the mass of white.

'Look! A Brochen Spectre,' he said trying to stop further questions. 'The locals say it's lucky to see one.'

Chirstie shrugged. 'It's just our shadow on the clouds.'

He sighed. 'I'm telling you the local folklore, I thought you might be interested. You were asking Dunkley a fair number of questions about it last night.'

'I was trying to be interested in the things he is interested in. I don't see why you won't discuss what must be public knowledge.'

Trewithick turned on her. 'Shut up, will you. I'm not going to gossip about my friend.'

He stalked into the clouds. His Spectre grew until it matched his six-foot of height. He shivered for a moment as he walked into it. He felt it wrap around him. He glanced back to make sure that Chirstie was following him.

She entered the cloud-fog.

Surrounded by a rainbow halo, she stopped a moment to assimilate the new data. 'Oh!' she said, looking at him.

'Fun isn't it?' He held a hand out in front of him and the hand gathered a multicolored halo.

She copied his gesture and smiled like a delighted child. She was much prettier that way, shame about all the slap she wore.

'The locals call this being blessed by the Spectre.'

She dropped her hand and rolled her eyes. 'God! People come up the silliest ideas. It's not as if they had the excuse of being unlettered yokels any more with the school for all. You can't tell me you believe in them?'

'I collect these stories, I'm sorry they bore you.' Trewithick walked on. Despite the low clouds, the trail was very clear. It would be impossible to miss the way if you knew the route. As the brightness faded so did the rainbow aura of the Spectre. The mist condensed on their faces and coats again.

'Oh!' she said. 'Oh! It's just clicked. You're *that* Sir Nathaniel Trewithick. I've seen your books in the windows of Borders.'

He hadn't said it to impress her. But now she walked close to him, skipping sometimes to keep up with his breathless, for her, pace. He just wished he was walking down alone.

The fog swirled around them. Sometimes he could see dark figures formed out the shadows, but when he started looking at them they vanished.

'Why did you start collecting them?' She looked up at him artlessly. 'Tell me some of the stories you collected. So what this about the Brochen Spectre. I thought you were just glorifying the credulous ideas of the locals. A couple of my friends did that when they bought their weekend homes in the country.'

Just to stop her mouth he opened his. 'The stories make it very lucky to walk through your Spectre, because it gathers the luck to you.'

As he paused for thought, she said, 'Did you get the knighthood for your writing?'

'It's a baronetcy,' he said.

'I beg your pardon?'

'It's not a knighthood, which is bestowed, I inherited the title, when I was seventeen.'

'I suppose you like to gather the folklore to debunk it,' she said. 'To show how far from our credulous past we have come in this enlightened age. Did you study history at University? So that you could give the history of...'

'Actually I studied theology, as did Dunkley. We both have our doctorates.' Last night he would have delighted in this feminine attention but now he wanted to tell her to shut up. 'Ah! Here's the turn I was looking for.'

'We should go straight,' she said.

'I beg your pardon.'

'Going straight on would get us down faster. I'm getting cold with all this damp and it's getting dark.'

Trewithick saw that she had forgotten to zip up her waterproof and her wool sweater was soggy.

'I'm afraid I don't know that path. We will have to take this turn,' he said. 'Zip up your coat for warmth.'

She looked down, then with shaking fingers she managed to get the zip fastened. 'For heaven's sake, this whole trip has been a complete disaster. I'm not staying out on this hillside a moment longer than I have to, just for your undue caution.'

'If the fog lifted, I might agree to a different route, but with this poor visibility it's best to stay on the path.'

'I'm going this way,' she said. 'It's too cold to stay out here.' She shivered again.

'Chirstie!' He tried to grab her and march her down the correct route, but she skipped sideways and ran down her chosen path. Around her colors of the spectre's blessing danced for a moment.

Trewithick pressed his hands against his eyes to push back the surge of anger that whispered he leave her to her fate. If she were right then she'd be at the pub before him.

Lowering his hands, he become conscious of being surrounded by the rainbow glow as well. He clenched and unclenched his fists. Leave her or go after the stupid bitch.

He spun to go on the path he knew, then stopped and looked at the glow. His training told him he was under an outside influence. His Spectre wanted him to take the regular path. Dunkley had said that those blessed would never run off cliff edges. Trewithick wondered if anyone came back and reported a Brochen Spectre curse.

'Chirstie! Stop!' He cupped his hands to his mouth and shouted again. 'Chirstie Leaker!'

There was a giggle in the mist.

He didn't dare run on a path that he didn't know--not in this weather, but he felt the urge to hurry.

The rainbow glow faded from his hands and a six-foot shadow grew out of the mist to stand in his way.

Trewithick took a deep breath and stepped through. The rainbow glow slapped back onto his skin.

With his heart pounding in his throat, he took another step along the path and another. His breath mixed with the mist surrounding him. It was nowhere near dark yet, but the clouds hid everything but the next step.

Again he put his foot down, slowly but that was all he could do.

Something suggested that he look down.

Taking a breath he dropped his gaze. On the edge of the path was a sweater. He crouched and gathered it up. It was soaked, but even in this weird light he could see it was Chirstie's. He laid it down again, he supposed that she had removed it because it was wet and she was cold.

The path angled steeply down. Maybe he would be below the cloud level soon and be able to see Chirstie. Stop her.

But you wanted her gone.

It took Trewithick a moment to be aware that it wasn't his thought. 'No! Well, Yes but No!'

She wanted to be away from you.

'It doesn't matter. Bring her back. Let me find her.'

She wanted to be away from the bore and in the warm. She has both.

'Let me find her!' He could feel tears running down his face.

Something brushed his cheek wiping away the trickle. *You offer your own water. But she is not mine.*

'Lead me to her, please!' He took another step. The cloud billowed out from his feet letting him see the rough sheep track.

'Chirstie Leaker! Stop!' In the next billow of mist he saw a shirt lying on path. He crouched again, it was an embroidered blouse. He recognized the primroses on the collar. What? Was she wandering naked through the fog?

He slid a hand into his pocket and picked out his phone. He needed help. Listening, he found he had a signal and dialed Dunkley's mobile. It was answered and in the background he could hear people talking.

'Alasdair!' he said.

'Nathaniel! What's the problem? Wait a moment, I'll go outside.' There was silence. 'Now, what's wrong?'

'She's run off into the fog. I can't find her.'

'I'll get the mountain rescue out. What was her coat color again?'

'I... I don't think she's got it on anymore. I've found other bits of her clothing.'

He heard Dunkley curse in Gaelic.

'I thought Spectres always led you right,' Trewithick said. 'Hers has taken her away from safety.'

'A Brochen Spectre is a reflection of who you are. Are you so certain in your own goodness? I would never listen to a Spectre.'

'Mine tried to stop me protecting her!' Trewithick hated that admission. 'I wanted to get rid of her. Now she's gone!'

'Stay where you are!' Dunkley said. 'Don't move! That hill has some bad scree slopes to fall into.' His Scots accent was marked under stress.

The line went dead. Trewithick put away his phone. He wasn't going to follow the last order. His ill-wishing had caused this, Dunkley had confirmed that. Leaving the blouse where it was, he continued his slow march along the path.

He heard singing.

'Chirstie! Chirstie is that you?'

He edged his way along the path, one little step, just as far as he could see. Then the clouds broke.

Chirstie danced naked on a ledge, humming a cheery song to herself. Even in the gloom under the clouds he could see her skin was blue with cold.

He increased his stride.

'Chirstie! Come back here.'

She danced as if he wasn't there. As he took a step towards her, she staggered closer to the sharp drop. Every movement had a rainbow contrail. Multiple rainbow shadows danced a stiff, cold dance with death as a partner.

He froze. 'Chirstie!'

Blind eyes finally saw him and laughed. 'It's the boring old fart!' Her voice was slurred.

'Chirstie you need to come here.' He shrugged out of his coat. 'You need to get warm.'

'Warm? I baking hot.'

'No Chirstie, you are cold. You need to get into this coat.'

He could see patches of blood on the rock where stone had cut into her soles. He tried taking a step towards her holding up the coat. Again the controlling Spectre made a funny little lurch edgewards.

'Chirstie come here, please!'

'What, are you still panting after me? You old dog! I saw you eyeing me last night. But what are you compared to Dunkley? Not even a poor second.'

'I'm everything you say, just come over here, please!'

She stood right on the edge. Her mouth opened wide and the rainbow aura poured out with her breath. For a moment it hung in the air around her head, then the aura faded into the gray of the clouds that gathered at her shoulder like a cloak

Her eyes opened wide. Her hands touched her naked body and she crossed her arms over her body in a classic Eve pose. Then she saw she was falling.

'Nathan! Help me!' she screamed.

She flung her arms out in supplication.

The movement flung her over, but for an instant, she caught herself, her fingers clawing frantically at the crumbling edge.

He charged over the ledge and flung himself flat on the ground to grab her hand. Their fingers brushed, curled together.

Trewithick flung his other hand round to catch her wrist, too late.

Her fingers slid out of his.

'NO!'

He heard her body rattle on the scree below. The heavy weight starting a slide of rocks.

Dizzy, he rolled away from the edge. He saw his Spectre was pulling him away.

His vision blurred.

He was still curled on the edge rocking when Dunkley's hounds found him.

Bite the Hand

Karl tried to frown, but his face had fixed into a smile.

'... then we got out our guns and paraded through the streets with them and shot all the baby girls,' John said. He shifted on the plush barstool and looked at the barman. 'Sam, think he might be under yet?'

The barman joined them, leaning over the warm wooden bar. 'What's your problem Karl? You seemed a bit upset when you arrived.'

Karl turned blurry eyes on the barman. 'Pardon?' Or at least that's what he wanted to say. It came out like a bubble.

'I think we solved your problems for you,' Sam said. He patted Karl on the shoulder, the movement exposing a tattoo of a dog running up his bicep.

John grinned at the barman. 'Should I take him over? I'm right about his aura, aren't I?'

'He's promised, and no else has claimed him. You take him to the master.'

'Hey, Karl?' said John

Karl tried to focus. 'Need to go,' he mumbled.

'That's right Karl,' said the barman. 'You go with John now.'

He felt John heave his arm over his shoulders. The man was strong for his skinny frame.

'Wanna stay here,' he managed.

'We're going to see Dennis, he's got a gift for you,' said John.

''s nice. Like presents.' Karl focused his eyes on John's arm. 'You gotta tat like the barman.' Part of Karl's mind was screaming. Something was really wrong here. ''s a dog.'

'It's a wolf.'

'Looks like a dog,' insisted Karl.

'It's a wolf. You'll understand shortly.'

One of the other young men in the bar joined John, and between them they half-carried Karl out through the door marked *gents*.

There was no door marked *ladies*.

'Where's the ladies?' Karl asked.

John laughed. 'You don't want the ladies, Karl. This is a man's club.'

'Put something in my drink,' Karl said.

'Yeah, we did,' John said. 'But you is promised. Any fool could see that, and I ain't no fool.'

Rain pattered on Karl's face. It had been raining when he left the second pub too.

* * * *

It was raining outside. He remembered he had left his coat at college.

Hugging the doorway, he glancing up and down the street to see if there was a taxi. There were none, but the only place a taxi could take him would be back to the College Halls of Residence. He was totally lost in East London--and couldn't care.

'Oy lad, get a move on, it's only a drop of rain. Some of us 'ave a thirst.'

Karl muttered 'Sorry' to the older man and stepped out into the mizzle. The street lamps washed the pavement and road with orange light. The raindrops made orange glass beads pattering down. They caught in his black hair and the trademark college ponytail directed them down the back of his neck.

* * * *

John and his friend shoved Karl into the back of a white van.

The roar of the engine burned into Karl's ears. He shook his head to try and clear his thoughts, but it made the darkness spin.

He lay still for remainder of the short journey. Then they dragged him out into the wet again. A door banged behind them and they were dry. Bare light bulbs stuck spears of light into his eyes.

His eyes wouldn't focus properly, but he could see the corridor was breeze-block. He was going up some stairs.

* * * *

He wanted to dash back up the stairs to the exorcism room and defend himself from the poor progress report that no doubt Mr. Dunkley had just demanded of Marishes.

A poor report he knew he didn't deserve. They weren't going to even let him fail the fifth year exam--Mr. Marishes would see that he never got to take it. He slammed a flat palm against the wall. Some of those defensive structures he could perform even better than Marishes. He took a deep breath but the oxygen only fed the fires of anger in his head.

Well, Marishes said he had a free afternoon. He would damn well take it. He stormed down the main staircase at the college and out into the lobby.

The doorman ran out from his room. 'Mr. Stempress...Stop! Mr. Dunkley needs...'

Drink, I need *a drink,* Karl thought.

Racing past the tube station with its newspaper stand, he ignored the placards shouting again about the gangs fighting it out over Hackney and Whitechapel. His mobile phone rang in his back pocket. Without even taking it out, he used a thumbnail to switch it off.

Well, Marishes had taught him defense; no one would find him until he wished to be found.

Karl wrapped London around him like a coat. He set his pace to match that of the brisk Londoners. He became one with them.

* * * *

His dad was going to be furious that he'd failed at the college.

What was *that* thought about? He tried to bring his mind into focus but the drug scattered his thoughts.

'What's that Karl?' asked John.

'NNnnnn!' Karl said. The drug invaded his whole body.

Invaded.

Space invaders. Like a man drowning in his own head he clung onto the idea.

Invaded.

Aim some guns at the invaders. Blast them out of the bloodstream. Get them before they land on your head.

Pop. Bang. Kapow.

* * * *

In the second pub Karl found what he was looking for. He got a pint and lots of change and immersed himself in a real, retro Space Invaders arcade game.

He came to himself when a band walked out into a clear area and started pounding out thumping loud music. He swallowed the last of his beer and accepted being driven from his refuge.

* * * *

Karl's head began to clear--enough so that he understood he should play drugged. He sagged between his two kidnappers. It didn't take much acting--any movement set the walls dancing.

'What have we here?' said a new voice.

Karl kept his head down. He concentrated as best he could on zapping the drug with Space Invader defenders.

'I saw him, Master Denis. His aura...' said John, eagerly like a puppy.

A hand, as gentle as Mr. Dunkley's lifted his head. Unlike Dunkley, this man stroked and probed his face. The touch made him shiver as the man looked around the edges of his soul.

* * * *

Once Mr. Dunkley finished grounding out the energies, he walked over to Karl. He leaned his stick against the wall and lifted Karl's head with his right hand. With cool hands he cupped Karl's chin.

Karl suppressed his shudder at the lover-like gesture, wondering what

108

would happen next.

With eyes unfocused, Mr. Dunkley stared around the edges of Karl's soul. Mr. Dunkley relaxed and released him.

'For a moment there, I was afraid something had crept past our defenses, convincing you to abate your enthusiasm. You are aware of your Father's fear for you, and how he almost begged us to accept you as a student here? So that you could learn how to keep yourself safe?'

'Yes, sir,' Karl said. His bitterness surfaced. 'I am kept aware of this.'

* * * *

Karl blinked, trying to clear his vision and focus on the dapper figure dressed in evil-villain black.

'A prize indeed John,' said Denis.

'He's called Karl,' said John.

Karl felt John preening under the praise.

'Well, Karl, I'm Denis Cameron. Would you like a gift?'

''s nice,' slurred Karl. 'Like presents.'

'Put him over there.'

John and the other man dragged Karl to a chair and dumped him while Denis watched.

'Good! Set out the howl and call in the rest of The Pack.'

The two young men left Karl alone with this Denis. Hair dyed black hanging in greasy rats tails down the back of the long black robes that he put on with great reverence.

Karl watched the man set up an altar of sorts. He unfolded a wallpaperer's table and spread out a black cloth over the top. Then he set out black candles stuck into what looked like black painted beer bottles. His lying of the athame on the center of the black cloth was theatrical. He put a brazier on the floor in front of the altar, lighting it with a barbecue lighter.

The fire danced up as Denis placed a grille over the brazier and set a pot of something over the flames.

It was all so poser-y.

If he hadn't seen what this could lead to, Karl would have laughed.

My mother, my stepmother and my uncle all destroyed their lives that way.

He'd seen real evil, and it didn't look like this. It looked just like your next-door neighbor, like your own mother--that's why it was so scary.

* * * *

Five minutes ago, the man in the circle had been a beast, spitting foul language, failing to cross the line drawn on the floor.

Now the man knelt, only dully aware of his surroundings.

'I'll take the penitent over to the asylum,' said Marishes. He turned to

Karl, barely concealing a sneer. 'You're free for the afternoon, Stempress.'

'Thank you, Mr. Marishes.' Karl bowed his head in acquiescence.

Penitent my foot, thought Karl, *these people don't want to lose their spirits. They cling to them and it destroys them.*

Mr. Dunkley, grounding out the energies, looked up, an eyebrow raised. 'Has Karl already visited the *treatment center*?'

Karl bit his tongue. He knew he had to keep his eyes lowered and mustn't answer.

Marishes pursed his lips. 'I haven't discovered in Stempress the major commitment needed for our work.'

* * * *

He supposed he'd better get out of here, before the big boys got back. Still feeling off from whatever they'd dosed his drink with, Karl pushed to his feet.

Denis swung around. 'Get back into that chair.' He pointed a stick, printed all over with Halloween skulls, at Karl.

It was all Karl could do not to snigger.

'Thanks for the invite, old man,' Karl said, his words still slurring a little. 'But I've got to get to another party.'

'Get back in that chair or I shall smite thee,' said Denis, waving his party wand about.

Karl held up his hands in mock terror. 'Ooooo, I'm afraid.'

'You are mine to claim,' spat Denis. 'By the seal that is set on your soul.'

Karl shrugged. How could he help it that his stupid mother had sold him into slavery to a cult? Before he was even thought of, she had promised her first-born son as a sacrifice.

Okay, so this Denis knew something because he could see his mother's curse.

Karl took a step towards the door, the walls swung, but less than before. 'I belong to me.'

'Pity the poor fool, who cannot accept his fate.' Denis swung his wand, Zorro-style, and shouted something in bad Latin.

Swathes of black smoke curled towards him from the candles, and Karl understood his mistake. He tried to run for the door but the drug tripped his feet.

He sprawled on the hard boards as the smoke became ropes of inky black.

'Thou hast set thine house of defense very high,' he whispered, trying to focus. *'A Thousand shall fall to the left of you and ten thousand at thy right hand,*

110

but it shall not come nigh thee.'

The drug, and the alcohol before that, had left his focus out of wack. The black smoke coiled around him in ropes that burnt where they touched the bare skin on his face and hands.

He was in real trouble.

Then he noticed that the coils did not tighten. He wriggled his hands and felt they could work free. He still had a chance.

From the stairs came the pounding of booted feet.

Denis strolled across and stared down at him. 'You will enjoy your new self better than you enjoy your life now.'

Nine men burst into the room, like eager puppies romping. There was lots of backslapping.

Denis looked towards them and scowled.

'You didn't give him enough rohypnol,' he said to the barman, Sam who was among them. 'He tried to get away.'

Sam shrank, and the other men slid away from him.

'I'm sorry Master Denis,' said Sam.

Denis flared his nostrils and stared down his nose at Sam. 'Never mind. Soon you will have the tenth member of your Pack and you can rip the throats out of Whitechapel.'

Denis turned away, and the backslapping became shoving. Not eager puppies then, more feral, starving puppies in front of whom a bowl of food has been placed.

With Denis's attention elsewhere, Karl wriggled his hand around to his back pocket. It was a tight squeeze, but he had to get to his phone. His fingers slid into the tight back pocket and he got a nail into the switch.

The leverage was wrong.

'Come my Wolves, greet thy maker.' Denis flung his arms wide.

As the sleeves on his robes dropped down, Karl noticed that Denis did not have the mark of the wolf on him.

The pack gathered around his feet, they curled up like dogs, which are ruled by terror, licking their master's boots.

And Karl began to wonder just what the sorcerer had in mind for him. From the pot on the brazier steam roiled out over the top.

That's when Karl grasped how much danger he was in. A wolf's head formed in the steam.

A gift! Oh Hell!

With what seemed superhuman effort he managed to flick the mobile on with his little fingernail.

He tried to switch it to buzz, but suddenly the frantic call of the mobile rang out through the warehouse.

With a petulant gesture Denis dropped his arms. 'Whose mobile is that?' he screamed. 'You've ruined the atmosphere!'

As the ringtone sang out, the wolf's head sank back into the water.

Karl couldn't get the thing switched off again. Following the sound of the ringer, the pack rolled Karl onto his face.

'Here, Master Denis, it's the new supplicant.'

Scowling, Denis waved an impatient hand. 'Chuck it in the corner--or better out the window. One of the street beggars can swap it for their shit.'

John switched it off and walked over to one of the long windows.

Karl tried wriggling after John--he needed the mobile. Two pairs of hands grabbed his shoulders.

'Let him see it go,' said Sam.

They lifted him up so he could as John eased the window open a crack and dropped the mobile onto the streets.

'No!' Karl screamed as his hope was thrown out with the rubbish. He sagged in his kidnappers' hands. He had needed the phone to call for help because he had shielded himself from detection.

Oh!

His eyes opened wide, but all he saw was the wooden boards. The hands dragged him towards the altar. Still woozy from the drug, he just wasn't thinking.

He forced his weaving brain to concentrate, then whispered, '*Who will rise up with me against the wicked, or who will take my part against the evil-doers?*'

The pack of men dropped him at Denis's feet.

'Now we'll have to start again,' he snarled. 'But fear not, you will get the gift of true manliness.'

'Some manliness.' Karl needed to slow down the ceremony. 'All I see are a bunch of boys in their *men's* club. No women allowed in here. Are you frightened of women?'

The pack growled and reached for him. He could see the claws extending from their hands.

He tried wriggling out of reach.

Once Denis saw that Karl was scared enough, he gestured the wolfmen back.

Denis leaned close enough to Karl that he could smell the mustiness of his greasy hair. 'I make allowances for a mummy's boy who has not received the Gift. We will break those ties to mummy's apron. The only uses my wolves have for a woman is to breed their strong pups. What would women know about the change? When they feel grumpy--they call it--once a month, they retire to bed with painkillers and a hot water bottle. They don't let the pain flow through them and cleanse them, purify them.'

He looked with pride at his pack and stepped back into his circle of what Karl now thought was blood.

He lifted his arms. 'Come! Greet your master!'

Reluctantly the men backed away from Karl. They turned away from him and resumed their awed positions around the feet of the warlock.

Denis lifting his arms, closing his eyes in the ecstasy of the moment. And Karl took his chance.

'*Cover me in the glory of thy cloke that I may walk among thy enemies unseen,*' he whispered. He rocked, and rocked, and finally got himself off his stomach. He continued over.

'They thought,' said Denis, beginning his sermon. 'They had wiped out wolves 400 years ago, but *we* will return them to their native shore.'

Quietly as he could Karl rolled to the side of the chair, where he had previously sat. Then he added, '*Thou hast set them their bounds which they shall not pass.*'

'We will set up such a howling that no one could fail to recognize their, your return.'

Denis started a chanting in his pig Latin.

The wolf's head in the steam grew clearer.

'Bring forth the supplicant.'

Karl held his breath as Denis opened his eyes to view--the blank spot where Karl had been. If he hadn't been pissing-his-pants scared he would have laughed at the warlock's expression of thwarted two-year-old.

'Where is he?' shouted Denis. 'Where is he?'

The men skittered around looking for Karl.

He could see the pack. In their human form they looked silly snuffling about the floor to make his scent, but he knew that the demons inside them would be able sniff him out.

'*Oh I am a stranger upon the Earth,*' Karl whispered.

Sam bayed, and scampered on all fours towards the chair. Karl tried to keep his panting breathing shallow so that he couldn't be heard. He had to believe that he wouldn't be found.

'Stupid dog,' shouted Denis. 'That's the scent of him from before.'

Sam scowled as he backed away from the chair. The rest of pack snuffled at the edges of the room.

'How did he get away?' screamed Denis. 'How could a drugged man break the bounds *I* had laid on him?'

Then Karl noticed that the Wolf's head was getting clearer as it hung in the air. The steam was roiling and spreading out like mist towards the nearest man--Denis.

With sudden wild inspiration, Karl knew what he had to do. But how?

'It must have been your fault Sam,' shouted Denis. 'You clearly didn't put enough drug in his drink. Did you *try* to sabotage the ritual? Wolves, one of your own wants you to fall to the Whitechapel lot. Do you think he's a spy for them?'

Eight men turned from sniffing the corners of the room and looked uncertainly between Denis and Sam.

And what about this pack business? Werewolves were, by their madness, lone wolves. How had Denis forced a pack on them?

However he had done it, Denis had forced them to work together. Now he was undermining the bond he had formed.

'*They encourage themselves in mischief and commune among themselves how they may lay snares,*' Karl breathed.

It didn't take much of a nudge. Sam grabbed the athame off the altar and stepped menacingly towards Denis. Denis scrambled behind the altar and grabbed one of the candleholder beer bottles.

Overhead, the Wolf elemental hovered.

Sam put a hand under the altar-table and flung it aside with a crash. The remaining candlestick holder clattered.

Denis backed to a wall and smashed the beer bottle against the wall to provide a weapon.

The bottle shattered all the way. Denis's tight grip collapsed about the shattered glass. Blood spilled between his fingers. The Pack stopped their snuffling for Karl. They could scent blood.

'NO!' Denis howled.

Sensing its way in, the wolf elemental billowed towards Denis. He held his arms over his head in a futile gesture, as it offered the blooded hand to the elemental. The elemental drank the blood and flowed into Denis.

And that made him the junior wolf around here.

And the pack knew it.

Sam batted him across the room. He crouched ready to pounce and rip Denis apart.

John stood in the way. 'You failed. I am the pack leader now.'

Sam scowled. In an instant he changed his plan and leapt for John. The other wolves circled. One of them pounced on his nearest pack member.

Hugging his injured hand, Denis began a slow crawl towards the door. Unwilling to give away his position, Karl wracked his brain for something to attract the attention of the other wolves, but the Pack bond had broken and madness of werewolves filled the room. They fought to remove potential rivals. The swirl of bodies filled the room. There was a scream of pain, and Karl saw the first one start shifting to manwolf. The limbs elongated, muscles pulling taut and joints wrenching into new places. The scream turned into a howl as the manwolf swiped at his rival. Others began to change.

John and Sam rolled on the floor. Elongating teeth snarled and snapped at throats. Claws ripped, trying to distract the other into giving way, without giving into the pain of the change.

Tucked away behind the chair, Karl was ideally placed to watch the brawl. The wolfman nearest Karl, sniffed the air.

Oh God! Don't let him smell me now! thought Karl.

The snuffling sounded louder, then the wolfman set up a howl and bounded towards the door--and the blood smell of Denis's shattered hand.

The outer door slammed open, and a man ran in. He pointed at the approaching wolfman.

'*His lightnings gave shine to the world,*' shouted the new man. Lightning poured out of his fingertips.

The wolfman jerked as his muscles responded to the electrical stimulus. Then he collapsed.

Karl recognized Mike Rider, who had helped sort out the mess in which his mother had left him. He lived in the East End of London.

Then Mr. Dunkley was in the warehouse. '*There shall go a fire before him and burn his enemies on every side.*' His hand threw fire at Denis, the nearest foe, who shrank from the conflict.

Marishes ran in behind Dunkley and squinted around the warehouse. With a sigh of relief, Karl dropped his shield.

'There he is,' shouted Sam.

Four wolves headed in Karl's direction. But Sam watched the newcomers.

His body melted into manwolf and he bounded over to the nearest window and ran through with his forearms over his face. The shattering glass sang a symphony, which drowned out the sound of the wolf fight and hunt.

Marishes sprinted across the room, his quarterstaff held before him. He stood over Karl and with both hands on one end he brought the staff down hard on the head of the nearest wolf.

In less time than Karl thought possible, the warehouse was full of college men. Bound as he was, all he could do was lie there while Marishes fought off wolves.

He held them off and took them down.

Denis was easily subdued. He sat nursing his hand in a corner. The remaining eight wolves fought like monsters.

Mr. Trewithick ran one wolf through, when Karl spotted another crept up behind him.

'Mr. Marishes,' he cried and pointed with his chin.

Still holding his staff with one hand, Marishes pulled out a gun and calmly aimed and fired.

The silver bullet tore into his chest, but the wolfman still pounced. With its last energy it ripped through Trewithick's sleeve with claws and fangs.

Trewithick batted it off with his sword. He quickly retired to the door and wrapped his silver crucifix around his arm like a tourniquet.

Then it was over: five dead wolfmen and four in silver chains.

Dunkley surveyed the scene then strode over to where Marishes stood over Karl.

They stared at each other.

Dunkley smiled coldly, and crouched in front of Karl. He cupped his hands around Karl's face. Now, after being handled by Denis, Karl could see there was nothing in there but kindness.

Staring into Karl's eyes Dunkley said, 'You know that smoke can't bind you.'

'Oh!' Karl said. He sat up as the inky smoke dissipated.

'Perhaps you could enlighten us as to how you ended up in this nest of werewolves?'

Karl studied his hands. They were grimy with the candle smoke. 'I went into a pub--the third one. And they saw my mother's promise in my aura. I was drugged and they brought me here. I managed to get the drug out of my system so I could think. Then I hid.' Then he remembered. 'Sir.'

Dunkley pursed his lips and nodded with respect. 'You didn't think to call fire or lightning to scare the water elementals, so that you could escape?'

Karl felt rueful. 'No, sir. I... I just waited to be rescued.'

'And how many other fifth years could have held off the whole pack with no help?' Marishes burst in.

'I know of none other,' Dunkley said, lifting his gaze to Marishes.

'I told you I have not stinted on his training.'

'Not in defense,' Dunkley said. 'But I think, before he enters the sixth year, perhaps he needs a few extra tutorials in offence?'

Marishes looked away. 'I was told to train him to defend himself. I did so.'

Dunkley nodded. 'And I agree you did that well. Could you take Trewithick to hospital? The Royal London's just down the road. And I think he will need a general exorcism with his stitches. I need to tidy up here.'

'Yes, of course.'

Marishes paused a moment and looked down at Karl. 'In my day, it was traditional for master to hand the student a symbol when they qualified for the rest of our study.'

With both hands, he held out his rune carved quarterstaff.

Karl blinked, but reached out to formally accept the gift. Nodding firmly, Marishes strode away.

'He actually thinks I did well. Why can't he tell me?'

'There are people who can't utter praise, without believing that those praised will get puff headed.' Dunkley smiled sadly. 'Unable to believe the damage they do by not issuing proper rewards.'

'And I'm going to be allowed to take the fifth year exam?'

'Karl, you healed the drug from your system. Anyone who understands self-healing is automatically passed into the sixth year--those are part of the deeper mysteries. It's true that no other fifth year could have held off the pack like that, but you need to realize there are those who think we should not have taken you just because your father begged for your safety.'

'They think I don't deserve a place here?' Karl said bitterly.

'I tested you myself, but some people will always believe what they want to believe. Come on. Let's get you back to Halls.'

He stood and held his hand out to help Karl up.

Karl gripped it, confidently.

Turn and Face the Night

Something hissed in the darkness.

'Eeeeeee-k!'

Josh froze against the cliff wall as a white shape sprang out of the bush and glided silently over him.

A shape drifted up the cliff and out of the gorge.

Panting, Josh pressed a hand against his racing heart. It was just an owl.

Memory of a lecture two weeks ago forced its way into his head. Romans believed owls to be the harbingers of death.

He pushed that nonsense aside and leant his cheek against the cold stone. Two more deep breaths and he managed to convince his adrenaline it was no longer needed.

He bent and snapped a twig from the hawthorn bush. The noise sounded sharp above the lullaby of seeping water. Glancing round, he took a breath and called light onto the finger-length wand. It flashed, setting sparks dancing on the glittering walls of the gorge.

Taking extra care not to disturb the local wildlife, Josh rounded a jutting edge.

There it was, a dark slash in the cliff walls, sucking in what little light there was from the half moon. A cave, the traditional entrance to the underworld.

He felt uneasy as his worn hiking boots scrabbled on the rock path.

Down here in the gorge, the world held its breath. Overhead, lustrous clouds, back lit by the moon, barely moved across what little Josh could see of the sky. A white shape drifted past, quartering the ground for prey. The rock walls of the gorge dripped with darker moss, and the river, which he could have jumped across, was a slick of oil.

'You're putting too much effort into that, Analay,' said Jeremy Wyndlyffe. 'Just a trickle or you'll end up worn out too soon.'

The distraction snuffed the light. It wasn't until Josh felt his fingernails dig into his palms that he noticed that his fists had clenched.

'I thought you were helping Karl?' Josh tried to sound pleasant.

'I wouldn't presume to comment on how Stempress sets up wards, but it's not as if the offender could get through the college tutors.' Jerry almost merged with the leprous stone of the cliff walls. 'I think he is wasting time putting up all that warding.'

'I was standing there as Mr. Trewithick asked him to,' Josh said.

118

'In my humble opinion, Stempress is so used to hiding and defense that he must fear an attack of any kind.'

Josh bit back his reply. The plum in Jerry's voice made him want to shout obscenities. Instead, he coaxed the twig to glow again and inspected the cave entrance.

Apparently, Tom loved Jess, in dayglo pink spray paint.

Above him he could feel the surge and sway of energies as Karl Stempress distorted the natural order into wards. The energies felt like the caress of a mother's hand over a child's fevered brow. They soothed away the fear and irritation.

Closer, he could see the lines of energy Jerry used to blend into the rock. It was an unfair advantage but Josh gave the older student a nod. He could feel Jerry tighten his lines. It just made him easier for Josh to find.

He grinned.

As Karl's layers of air and darkness settled back into the earth, Josh felt like something in him had died.

A few moments later, Karl joined them at the cave entrance. The long staff Karl had received from his former tutor clicked against the stone.

On arrival, Karl touched a hand to the virulent declaration of love. With a bemused smile, his hand traced out a sausage shaped object scratched deep into the surface. Then snatched it away as he examined the entrance more closely.

Josh bent to look. He could make out letters gouged next to the drawing. 'What does *mansueta tene* mean?'

From the darkness Wyndlyffe snorted, like a braying donkey.

'It's just some Roman graffiti.' While not as plummy as Jerry's, Karl's rounded vowels bore the same stamp of a public school education.

'Romans again.' Josh looked up for a glimpse of the owl.

'A bit further back there's a quarry,' Karl said. He eyed the slit in the cliff face. 'Do we have to go down there, do you think?'

'I would say so,' Jerry said.

Karl didn't even glance towards where Jerry's voice emerged from solid rock.

'Well, if we're going...' Karl said. He glanced at Josh. 'Want to stay up here and guard the entrance?'

'I want to see the Cave Art,' Josh answered. 'Mr. Dunkley lectured us second years on this cave last week.'

Both Karl and Jerry shared an amused glance. Josh flushed. Was his admiration for Mr. Dunkley a joke?

119

A swirl of air, and Karl's staff phosphoresced. He led the way into the slit. Josh chucked away his hawthorn twig. The fading glow illuminated *Helena amatur a Rufo*. He ducked in immediately after Karl, letting the other fifth year take the rear guard. The thin slit narrowed and the three men had to ease their way sideways to get further in.

'So tell me again,' Josh whispered. 'If the tutors have it all in hand, what're we doing here?'

It was something Josh often wondered. What was a lad from a Barnsley state school doing among all these sons of the public school system?

'I expect,' Karl whispered back. He lifted his staff higher, sending shadows dancing over the walls. Teeth hung down from the ceiling as the entryway emerged into a larger chamber. 'From the way the students have been scattered over the Sacred Sites in this district, the tutors are getting us out of the way while they hunt down the baby's kidnapper.'

The whispered words filled the trapped air with susurration.

'Why would one of those East End Wolves come all the way out here? We're in Derbyshire.' Josh wrinkled his nose against the cold, stale air--almost as bad as an underpass on a Saturday night.

Karl shrugged. 'It's on the run from us. It had to go somewhere.'

'I've said before, that man will never get through the tutors,' Wyndlyffe interrupted.

Rubbing his fingers against the glazed sheen on the stone Josh said, 'They could have just sent us down the pub.'

'We can dream.' Karl said. 'I think I'm going to do my dissertation on the old wives tales people think work to banish their demons.'

'Good, you can tell me how these right odd ideas get started,' Josh said.

'Because the evil creatures that infest them--' Wyndlyffe started.

'That's an easy one: desperate hope,' Karl interrupted.

'Hope for what, exactly?' Wyndlyffe demanded.

'Oh come on! We've been in the same classes. You know the common belief among the wolf fraternity that biting an innocent baby will transfer the wolf demon to the baby,' Karl said.

'But a baby can't be freed of an infestation. It's got no life experience. We'd have to...' Josh trailed off, shocked.

'That's why our tutors want to get to the baby before he's infested,' Karl said. 'I expect the kidnapper really believes that he wants to be free. They don't know what it's like afterwards.'

The damp chill of the cave settled on Josh's shoulders. He shivered, tugging his coat closer around his chest. He felt Karl pulling the energies of the earth around him to keep warm. Josh wished he was strong enough to do that sort of thing, but felt comforted by the subtle tingle that stroked through his hair.

Karl strode into the main chamber, the moving light casting shadows that made the stalagmites and stalactites shift, like they were about to chomp down. 'Okay, let's find a spot to camp.'

'Where's the cave art?' Josh edged over to the wall and peered into the gloom.

Karl brought the light over to him. On the other side of the cave, Jerry had summoned some light. He sprawled on a flat stone. Behind him a large stalactite bowed over the stone, like a grief-hunched figure over a grave.

Josh gave himself a mental shake and tuned out the way the two lights shifted the settled energies in the cave. He felt the calling. His head jerked that way and his feet had taken two steps before he got them under his rule again. Karl looked at him sharply.

'I think it might be over here,' Josh said, gently touching the calling again.

It was as quiet as dust drifting in a sunbeam.

Old, the call smelled of dust and centuries. It led to a wall. Josh held out a hand above the surface. In the air he traced a bison.

'What is it?' asked Karl.

'An old call of hunter to prey.'

'Hunting magic,' Jerry said from across the room. The roughness in his voice set the energies trembling. The echoes sent shivers of repulsion down Josh's spine.

Josh looked up and saw Karl watching him closely.

Josh shrugged. 'There's not much there now.'

'How about we get comfy?' Karl said. 'We've got to stay here until daybreak anyway.'

Josh could see he had produced a hip flask. Leading the way to the flat stone that Jerry had chosen, he offered it to Josh.

'Honestly,' said Wyndlyffe. 'We're supposed to stay alert.'

'And I thought you knew nothing would get through our tutors.' Karl grinned. 'Want a nip? To keep out the cold?'

With his boots Josh scraped a patch of floor clear of centuries of muck and settled down with his back against the bowed over stalagmite. 'What--?'

Pain shot through the darkness. A black hole ate at the bright heart of the countryside. Josh screwed up his face against the gnawing ache eating into his guts.

From somewhere close by someone cried out with the black heat of pain.

Calmness spread over him from a cool point on his forehead. The security of Karl's aura covered Josh.

Karl had a hand on his head. The staff leant against the wall casting its protection against the non-light.

'What's wrong?' Karl asked.

'There's Nothing out there,' Josh whimpered.

'Well, we don't have to worry then,' Wyndlyffe said.

Karl shot him a silencing glance. 'Care to rephrase that statement?'

'There's nothing moving out there,' Josh said. He could feel empty darkness shifting through the living rock. It sucked at the life and spat out death.

'You're trying to tell me something, Josh, it's just we're not speaking the same language.' Karl frowned, his eyes going blank. 'There's nothing got through my wards.'

'That's right,' Josh said. He grabbed for Karl's coat. '*Nothing's* got through your wards and *it's* moving down here.'

'I think something's gone in his head,' Wyndlyffe said.

'Shut up, Jerry,' Karl said. 'I need to know what he's talking about. Can't you see that he's having a vision? His skin's all clammy.'

Wyndlyffe touched Josh's wrist. Josh wanted to pull away, but the contact didn't last long.

'I didn't know he was a visionary.' Wyndlyffe fished in his pocket and pulled out a packet of glucose tablets. He handed them to Karl.

'I didn't know, but I've sort of guessed since I've been working with Mr. Trewithick,' Karl said. 'Josh... Oh! *he* sees things differently.'

Terror gripped at Josh's stomach. 'It's moving in here.'

The cave acoustics magnified the squeak of his terror, echoing and doubling it.

As he finished speaking, Karl stuffed two tablets in Josh's mouth.

The warmth melted on his tongue and spreading to the joints of his mouth, cutting through the icy terror in his head. He gasped in relief.

'Get ready for a possible attack,' Karl said to Wyndlyffe.

'I think we should find out what the ass is saying first.'

A scuffle sounded at the entrance to the cave. Karl snuffed the light on his staff. Between them, he and Jerry grabbed Josh and retreated to the edge of the cave behind some stalagmites.

A darker shadow stalked into the center of the cave. His torch flashed around, but failed to pick out the three in the corner.

'Bloody hell,' Karl whispered. 'He's carrying a baby. The perp got through the tutors.'

Wyndlyffe pressed his mouth close to Karl's ear. 'Get outside and call the tutors. The phone won't work in here. I'll engage it. I'm best at attack.'

'No!' Josh tried to scream his whisper. 'It will eat you. It eats life.'

Wyndlyffe rolled his eyes at Josh's concern. 'I think you need to rest while the big boys sort out this problem. Call the tutors, Stempress.'

The whispered conversation set rolling echoes around the cave.

The man twisted, waving his torch around as he tried to see where the noise was coming from.

Josh watched as the man-shaped black hole stood his lantern torch on the stone slab and laid the baby next to it. It lay very still for a baby and was deathly quiet. Josh remembered girls from school who'd got knocked up; the babies had always been screaming.

The bent-over stalagmite inspected the offering as the intruder set a bag down.

'Do you think the baby's dead?' Josh mummered.

'Let's hope not.' Karl hauled Josh up with his left hand under his arm. 'You need to come with me.'

Wyndlyffe strode out.

In the center of the cave, the intruder turned to face Jerry. The blackness that hung around him sucked at Josh's eyes. The shadow man pulled every hint of warmth and hope into himself. Josh's head spun and he tried to look away.

Wyndlyffe raised his hand. '*For the arms of the ungodly shall be broken.*'

'Fool,' hissed the shadow man. 'You can't touch me with your silly toys.' He charged at Wyndlyffe.

'*Shall not thy wrath burn like fire!*' shouted Wyndlyffe as he dived to one side.

The shadow man kicked at Wyndlyffe's side.

Staggering a bit, Wyndlyffe rolled back to his feet.

With the intruder's back turned, Karl picked up his staff and maneuvered Josh to the cave entrance.

Josh looked back to the stone slab. A spark of aura hung about the child. 'The kid's alive.'

'You can see it?' Karl said. 'I've never been good at auras.'

They sidled up the tunnel to the outside, coats scraping on the jagged walls.

The less intense darkness outside the cave welcomed them. Josh could breathe again.

Karl punched the speed dial on his phone. There was no wait. 'Sir!

The kidnapper is here, at the cave. The baby too.'

As Karl dropped his phone back into his pocket, Josh said, 'But I don't think we're dealing with one of the left-over wolves.'

'Go on.'

'He's got a sort of anti-aura.' Josh waved a hand about uncertainly. 'There's nothing in him at all.'

'A warlock, then?' Karl frowned. 'I've got to get back in and help Jerry. You wait here.' He pressed the packet of glucose sweets into Josh's hand.

Josh leaned against the cliff wall. The warmth from the previous glucose tablets was fading. He stuffed another one into his mouth. Finally he understood.

'He's an empty soul.'

'What?' demanded Karl, turning back.

'He's been possessed and the demon was removed. He's mad,' Josh said. 'None of our stuff can touch him, he's theologically dead.'

'What do we do?' asked Karl.

'What you asking me for? You're the bloody fifth year!'

Karl nodded firmly, then hurried back into the dark cave.

Josh followed more slowly. He did not want to be doing this.

'Jerry! Physical force! Not practical theology,' Karl shouted.

Wyndlyffe glanced at Karl, then shouted. *'Tremble in fear before his--'*

The shadow man backhanded Wyndlyffe across the head and Wyndlyffe flew back. They heard the crack of his head on the cave wall.

The headache caused by his life being drawn off by the shadow man was intensifying. Josh dug his fingers into his temples and slid down the stone.

'Any more baby witch-finders here to challenge me?' the shadow man almost sang his gloating words. He stepped back to the stone slab and produced a drum and a cymbal from his bag.

Karl frowned. 'I know that voice.'

He stepped forward and lifted his staff.

The shadow man drummed a heartbeat rhythm. The cave caught the pulse and the rock seemed to fill with life.

Josh grabbed Karl's coattail, trying to see around the jagged lines of pain in his vision. 'Practical theology won't work.'

Karl adjusted to what Josh recognized as a quarterstaff grip. Karl sidled into the circle, and Josh huddled by the entryway, ice churning in his stomach. He pressed a hand over his mouth to keep the bile down. The stone behind his back felt warm from his body heat. His head pounded. He twisted to lay his forehead against the cool stone.

But it wasn't cool.

The stone walls beat with life warmth--like skin.

Josh surged to his feet, backing away. He leant forwards and touched it with a delicate finger. The heat was subsiding, but it was warm--the way jet warmed in the sunlight.

In the center of the cave the kidnapper stood beating on the drum. It felt like they were in the stomach of a living creature, and Josh could see the lines of energy running to his fingertips pulsing with the heartbeat.

Karl had been right in his guess. This was a warlock and there was a creature here to be summoned.

'I remember you,' said the warlock. 'You're the Gift Untaken, the one who destroyed my pack in Hackney. You're even better than the babe.' He stepped back and raised his arms again. 'Come to me creature of the night and light the skies with this offering.'

'Dennis,' Karl said. 'I defeated you then. I can now.'

The drumbeat intensified, filling the cave with the sound of a racing heart.

Josh snatched his hand away from the suddenly scalding stone. The heat jarred through the pain in his head. His heart raced in time to the beat, his body responding to the threat with terror.

And the earth moved.

Karl staggered as the ground rolled under his feet. Karl was the best at defense that the college had turned out in years. He could handle anything a creature could call up. He hammered the iron foot of his staff on the ground and it stabilized. As the creature distracted Karl with its attack, the warlock flung aside his drum and jumped Karl.

'I'll have you for my offering,' he hissed.

Karl whacked his staff down onto the Warlock's head.

The crack echoed through the cave and the Warlock dropped. Dark blood dripped to mingle with the dirt on the cave floor, but as he touched the ground the head wound healed and he surged up again.

Karl dodged out of reach.

The deeper darkness of the cave echoed back the drumbeat, but it was fading.

Josh knew he should help, but he couldn't. He hung back near where Wyndlyffe sprawled unconscious. The void within the warlock sucked at him. He turned his gaze away from the warlock and the drain slowed. His brain started to work again.

Where are the tutors? thought Josh.

He bit the back of his hand as he watched, trying not to feel the draining shadow.

Then his other sight surged up--he could barely control it. Lines of power ran from the stalagmite that bent over the stone slab where the baby lay.

The stalagmite had straightened. It throbbed with power, accepting the worship of the men fighting.

Water from the ceiling began to drip on the baby. The torchlight shone on the slab and the baby's skin slowly went gray.

It was turning the baby to stone.

Josh knew he had to do something. He was the only one who could see what the creature was doing.

Karl swung his staff at knee level. The warlock jumped, but Karl expected that and whacked his knee in a quick return.

Again the creature in the cave healed him, but more slowly as the drumbeat faded.

Panting, Karl tried a head attack.

Gathering the powerlines to him, the warlock waved his hand.

Solid air punched Karl in the stomach. Karl collapsed to the floor, clearly winded at least.

The warlock dived for his drum. His fingers pattered the hypnotic heartbeat.

Concentration shot, Karl began to weave in time to the rhythm. He rocked back and forth on his knees.

The warlock swaggered to where Karl tried to lift his staff, then kicked it out of Karl's weakened grasp.

Where were the tutors?

Josh slipped his hand into his jacket pocket. Swallowing hard, he said, 'Physical is the only way.' He pulled out his cast iron knuckle-duster. The iron wouldn't help here, but it was solid on his fist.

'Karl!' he shouted. He had to break the beat. The noise echoed round the chamber. *Karl! Karl! Karl! Karl!*

'Get back,' Karl gasped.

Stepping over Wyndlyffe's legs and wishing the prat wasn't there to break his stride, Josh ran at the warlock. 'Karl! Get the baby out into the air. Your strength is in defense.'

The anti-aura and the shadows in the warlock's soul sucked away at the hope in Josh's heart. The soothing heartbeat made Josh sleepy. He staggered and fell to his knees. The warlock laughed.

'You baby witch-finders are a mess,' he said. 'Are you going to come at me one at a time?'

He strolled towards Josh, fingers tripping lightly over the skin, just enough to keep up the mesmerizing rhythm.

Josh raised his head. 'You need to be careful. You don't know what you're dealing with here.'

'That's a joke! I've been working with spirits for years,' the warlock said. As he moved closer Josh could see that was a boast, the man didn't look any older than he was.

'Earth elementals?' Josh gasped.

'Earth, air, water, fire, what's the difference,' the warlock said.

'A great deal,' Josh said. 'For instance, if you knew anything about this elemental you'd know that a baby was the wrong offering.'

The warlock shrugged. 'A baby is always a good offering.'

'To a fertility god?' Josh laughed. 'You should have brought the mother and it doesn't want her dead either.'

'It's no matter. This one called me. It can give me back what I lost. What *he* stole from me.' A finger jabbed at where Karl... had been lying. 'Where is he?'

The warlock spun around. The baby was gone from the slab, only the lantern torch remained to light the gap.

'Where's my sacrifice?'

Josh pushed up from the ground. Standing, he took a step toward the warlock. 'All safe in the air.'

The warlock dashed to the slab. He grabbed the torch.

Head down, Josh ran in full tilt, determined to make the most of his momentum. He punched the knuckle-duster into the warlock's solar plexus.

The man dropped the drum.

Josh smashed his foot through the casing and kicked it to the wall.

'No!' the warlock howled. The cry echoed around the chamber. 'That's how you control the elemental. Get the cymbal! End the ceremony!'

He tried crawling on his knees away from Josh, towards the brass cymbal that lay in the center of the chamber.

Josh gave him a donkey kick in the shoulder and the warlock slammed up against the stalagmite.

Coughing, the warlock dropped to his knees on the stone slab.

Water dripped down on him from above.

The black anti-aura sucked at him but Josh held the man against the stalagmite, under the steady flow.

The black dyed hair became streaked with gray: solid gray. Tears of stone ran down his face. From the ground, liquid-looking stone glaze flowed over the man's knees, holding him in place.

The warlock screamed. He smashed his hand against the glaze. His fist stuck.

'Help me!' the warlock screamed. *Help me! Help me! Help...*

'I don't know how,' Josh said. He watched as more water dripped from above.

The warlock tried pulling his arm away with the other hand. It too became coated with the stone glaze.

'I only wanted a spirit back, after you people ripped my soul away. I wanted to stop feeling so empty, alone. It called me. It told me it could fill me. Help!'

Josh crouched and hammered at the growing glaze with his knuckle-duster. A clatter of falling stone, and Josh saw he had smashed the warlock's arm off. It had turned to stone all through.

Horrified, Josh backed away.

The warlock stared at where the bottom half of his arm had been. 'Don't take me! Free me, I'll get your sacrifice back!'

Behind him, Josh heard a scrabbling. Two gray shadows streaked into the cave, closely followed by a panting Dunkley. The dogs circled the frozen warlock.

Dunkley lifted his hands. Josh could feel a draft from the entry passage as the tutor tried to summon air, but surrounded by the walls of the cave, the air was sluggish.

'Help me!' the warlock screamed. 'The cymbal.'

Josh dived for the cymbal and crashed it against the nearest wall.

Joined with the warlock's screams the noises echoed off the walls. They reverberated against the ceiling, echoed and redoubled.

Josh dropped the cymbal. He tried to block out the sound with his fingers. The wolfhounds flattened their ears and backed out of the cave, snarling.

And Dunkley sweated as he tried to fight back the petrification.

Josh turned away as he saw the stone glaze creep up over the warlock's neck. He bit into his hand to distract him from the urge to throw up.

The screaming stopped.

Dunkley bowed his head and the air in passageway stilled. Josh stared at the new stalagmite. It didn't look much like a kneeling man. Josh wasn't an innocent. With the knees like that and the body straight up...

Giggling would probably be considered an inappropriate, hysterical reaction.

Josh flicked a glance at Dunkley, then away, as he saw defeat in his hero's eyes. All desire to laugh fled.

Behind the new stalagmite, the old one had slumped over again.

'Where's Wyndlyffe?' Dunkley asked. 'I thought he was with you and Stempress.' *Press, press press!* Even that sound was caught by the cave acoustics and magnified.

Josh glanced around the chamber. Wyndlyffe lay where he had fallen, mouth slightly open, and eyes staring.

Following the gaze, Dunkley strode across the chamber. He knelt beside Wyndlyffe. Josh watched as the tutor became still. Fingers gently pressed on the neck of the student. Then Dunkley bowed his head. His hand brushed over the eyelids to cover the dead eyes.

He died, and I didn't even notice, Josh thought. He pressed his hand to his mouth, but tears leaked over his fingers. His other hand found Wyndlyffe's packet of glucose tablets in his pocket. *But he's dead!*

He stepped aside as Dunkley lifted the body and led the way out of the cave.

Dying to be Thin

Josh wished he spent less of his time in churchyards. Across the road, a local electrical shop had all the televisions in the window on the same channel, showing a pink commercial, involving teen dolls and all the spin-off merchandise. A reminder that life still happened out there while he was learning to deal in death.

Dangling his legs over the edge of the sarcophagus, he nursed his mug of tea and listened to a man and woman arguing further down the path.

Butterflies darted into the air, from where they had congregated around the edge of puddle. They were a new sort to him, but as he had goofed off in biology he was lucky if he could tell the difference between a Cabbage White and a Peacock. They fluttered up in a frantic vortex of colors, startled as the two people came into view.

The couple looked faintly familiar, and were about his age, but he was sure he'd never met them before. He found the déjà vu that grew with training odd, but he studied them surreptitiously.

The woman stepped around the puddle and wrinkled her nose. 'Why can't dog owners be more responsible? This is a graveyard.' She turned away.

Josh studied the stained glass in the church window, to show he wasn't paying them any mind, but the woman stopped.

'Is that the vicarage over there?' she asked him.

Another of these lah-di-dah public school voices--his Mam would have it that he was getting one.

'Over back,' he said, nodding at a path through the gravestones.

'Thank you.' The woman returned to her companion. 'We've still got to report it, Philip.'

Philip sighed. 'Look Penny, it's not that I...'

The gate to vicarage squeaked open and Mr. Trewithick walked through. Even the weak spring sun seemed to show his bones; he looked shockingly ethereal next to the bulky vicar, Mr. Willoughby.

'And has he even been baptized, I want to know?' Willoughby growled.

Josh jumped to his feet, without spilling his tea, and grinned. 'I am now, sir.'

Mr. Willoughby scowled--a scowl that Josh remembered from when he had failed an RE exam.

'Do you know your mother stormed into school, accusing me of corrupting you?'

'She's not so keen on me reading Theology.' Josh hid his smirk under a sip of cooling tea. 'Think these folks want to talk to you.' He swigged the last of the tea and set the cup down.

Mr. Trewithick looked resigned as he stepped around the young couple. 'Try not to be so provoking, Josh,' he said in an undertone.

Josh shrugged. 'So why are we here?'

They walked towards the puddle to give the vicar an illusion of privacy with the young couple.

Even more butterflies danced on the sunbeam that strayed through the yew cover.

'Mr. Willoughby believes the town epidemic of measles is nothing to do with do with low uptake of vaccine.'

Now he was closer, Josh could see the dog shit bordering the puddle that had the woman wrinkling her nose. Why were the pretty flitters landing right there?

'Feverflies,' said Mr. Trewithick nodding at the butterflies. 'It's an old country name for them. Apparently there has been a plague of them this summer.'

'And here I was thinking it was nice to see them back, after all the wet summers we've been having.'

Mr. Trewithick grinned. 'I'll show you the summoning and then...' He broke off looking over Josh's shoulder. Josh turned.

'Excuse me, Trewithick,' said Mr. Willoughby, walking towards accompanied by the young couple. 'I think this one's for you as well.'

Mr. Trewithick turned to the couple. 'How can *we* help you?'

With a final glare at Josh, Willoughby retrieved the mug and stomped away muttering, 'It seems like you accept anyone these days. They were pickier when...'

Josh stuffed his hands in his pockets.

The couple looked uncomfortably between the retreating vicar and Josh. The young woman made a decision. She turned to Trewithick.

'You see I was staying with a friend, and she's been taken to hospital. She's wasting away--almost like when she was in school with me and had anorexia. Chloë swears she's eating properly, and I've seen Chloë's younger sister playing with fairies. Oh, this sounds all so silly. I'm Penny Bailey, by the way, and this is Philip Stempress.'

Josh felt his eyebrows go up. 'Karl's brother?'

Philip smiled slightly. 'Yes, and his half sister, Penny. Do you know Karl?'

'Yeah!' said Josh. 'He's meeting us later.'

'I'm Trewithick, your--'

'Karl's new tutor?' Penny asked.

Trewithick nodded.

'Well I hope you teach him to--'

'Penny,' said Philip.

Penny glared at him.

Philip continued, 'At least you'll believe Penny's wild tale. She thinks Chloë's younger sister is getting the fairies to make Chloë ill.'

Trewithick studied Philip. 'Have your burns recovered?'

'Yes, thank you.' Philip flushed.

Josh flicked a glance between Philip's defiance and Trewithick's amused understanding.

'Since you are here, I can take your report,' said Trewithick. 'Rather than wait for Karl to receive it during the Easter vacation.'

'There's nothing to report,' shouted Philip.

Penny put a hand on his arm but he shook it off.

'I got caught in a wildfire on the moors--that's all!'

'Josh.' Trewithick smiled sadly. 'Take Miss Bailey and look for evidence of these fairies. I think I need to talk to Philip.'

'I said nothing happened,' said Philip.

'Then tell me how you perceived the fire.'

Josh beckoned Penny over. 'Come on, then, let's get out of their way. Your brother needs to have a chat with Mr. Trewithick.'

'He's not my brother,' said Penny, flushing.

Josh frowned. 'Umm...'

'Karl is my half-brother, Philip is Karl's half-brother but my cousin.'

Josh scratched his neck. 'Step-brother?'

Penny sighed. 'Karl and I share the same mother. Philip and Karl share the same father. My father and Philip's mother were siblings--'

Josh held up a hand. 'Karl said his family got complicated. We need to get going. So what's this about fairies? Little girls often play with fairies at the bottom of their garden.'

'Not when they get to fourteen.'

Josh pursed his lips. 'Okay, I see where you're coming from. Is this place far?'

'We can take my car.' A zippy red sports coupe flashed a greeting as she pointed the key at it. She grinned as Josh stroked a hand over the paintwork and added, 'There's no point in having a rock star for a guardian if you can't ask for a good car for your birthday.'

'Is he adopting anymore kids?' Josh climbed into the passenger side.

He saw butterflies flying off, hopefully to more salubrious locations.

The engine purred into life and Penny pulled away from the kerb.

They drove in silence until Penny took a left into a posh neighborhood. Josh scrubbed his hands over the dirty knees of his jeans.

'Is it that house?' He pointed to a house further down the street. A sludgy gray-brown miasma of hatred dripped from the eaves. He pressed a hand over his mouth.

'Are you okay?' asked Penny. She stopped the car away from the house.

'I'll be fine.' Josh pressed his fingers into his temples and tried to See what lay beneath the slime. 'I'll need to get closer.'

He opened the car door and slipped onto the pavement. Blinking to clear his vision, he took a step forward, but the sweltering heat of anger surrounding the house drove him back.

Penny walked around the car. The hatred caused a mirage and she seemed to waver in and out in of his Sight.

'Are you coming then?' she asked irritably. She turned and looked back at him. 'What's wrong with you? You gone all white.'

'Unlock the car,' he stammered.

'What?' Penny frowned. Then she shrugged and flicked the button on her key chain.

The flashing lights on the car stabbed into his eyes. He hung on the car roof and tried to get the door open.

'What is wrong with you?'

Her words struck into his skull like sharp hammer blows. He fumbled for the handle. He tugged it open and almost fell into the seat. The wavering vision cut out as soon as he was insulated from ground.

'Well aren't you coming? I thought you were going to look around for Mr. Trewithick.'

'I can't,' he said. He reached into his pocket and stabbed the speed dial button. He held the phone to his ear, then he hung up. 'Mr. Trewithick's phone is turned off.' He could feel the acid tang of fear in his throat. 'He never turns off his phone.'

'Huh? I don't understand.' Penny stared at the house, squinting slightly as if trying to see what he could see.

'I can't go near that house without extra protection,' said Josh. 'Karl! He's the best at warding.' He checked his watch. 'Can you take me to the station? He's on the 16.40 train.'

'Oh God! Do I have to?'

'Well you could drop me a bit further away from that house and I could walk,' said Josh. He shuddered at the thought of getting out of the car anywhere nearby here. He actually regretted that there were pretty butterflies here. A popular belief held that animals and insects could sense aura; it was certainly false here. Josh opened the car window, he felt stuffy and ill from the house.

Penny got into the driver's seat. 'Fine! I'll take you to the station. What happened to you?'

'I tend to go a bit funny around the bad stuff, still.' He glanced at Penny's set face. 'Why don't you like your brother?'

'Half-brother,' said Penny, as she pulled away from the kerb. She executed a three point turn and added, 'Because when he was fifteen, and I was thirteen, he cast a love spell on me and his brother Philip. It hasn't gone away yet.'

Four pink-coated teenagers minced down the pavement on high heels. One of them held up a teen-doll and circled the doll's waist with thumb and finger. The girl wore layers of make-up leaving a waxy sheen on her face.

'...like Dorian Grey,' the teen said, stuffing the doll away and unwrapping a chocolate bar.

'Does it hurt? I mean Chl--' demanded one of her friends.

The first teen interrupted. 'She didn't eat enough.'

... well, they didn't concern him. Josh looked away from the girls and traced a finger over the car door. 'Doesn't work that way, you know.'

'What?' Penny glanced at him, then back to the road. 'It certainly has.'

Josh shrugged. 'I know I'm only in my second year, but I've learnt a bit.'

In the wing mirror, Josh saw the visions in pink turn into the driveway of the house he couldn't even think about approaching.

'Oh and how does it work, then?'

Josh looked back at Penny with a raised eyebrow at her tone. 'The most likely reason for the continuation of the love spell is that you f-- I mean consummated the er...m desire.'

Penny turned bright red. 'You mean that the gentlemen of the college all think... But we were only thirteen!'

Josh hid his grin. 'Ain't going to bother me sweetheart, I'm from Barnsley.'

'But we didn't, we didn't.' It was almost whispered. 'I rather gathered you weren't the usual intake.'

'And your half brother's the only one who doesn't act like I'm a slug to be scraped off their shoes.'

'I'm sorry.' Penny stared at the road. 'Isn't there anything else that could have happened?'

'You won't like the other option any better.'

'Go on, ruin the rest of my day.'

'That one or other of you is re-casting the love spell when ever you meet.'

Penny turned down a side street. She pulled into a parking space outside the wooden clad station and glared at the peeling paint.

Josh checked his watch then opened the door. 'I'll go and meet Karl.' He wove through parked cars to the entrance, glancing back he saw her resting her head on the steering wheel.

The station was unattended. On the platform, a passenger frantically stabbed a button on the self-service ticket machine as the lines hummed. A ticket rewarded his efforts as the train arrived.

A lanky man swung onto the platform. Karl looked a lot like Penny with their dark hair and eyes. Philip's coloring was lighter. Karl caught sight of Josh and hitched his backpack over his shoulders.

'Thought I was meeting you at the vicarage?' Karl held out his hand. They gripped wrists and Karl whacked Josh happily on the back.

'There's a bit of trouble,' said Josh. 'I've lost Mr. Trewithick.'

'Hey?' Karl turned serious.

'I've got a lift for us.' Josh hitched a thumb at the exit as the aging diesel train groaned away from the platform.

Standing under the awning, Karl flicked a glance at Josh. 'You've never got Penny to help out.' He nodded at the sports car. He waved cautiously at Penny and the boot of the coupé smoothly lifted.

Karl strode across and dumped his pack inside. He unhitched his staff from the side and closed the lid.

'You didn't have to slam it,' said Penny.

'I'll crawl in the back, should I?' said Josh.

'It's better if I go in the back. Pen would be hitting me instead of driving if I sat in the front.'

'You don't have to be nice to me any more, Josh explained it all to me.' She turned to Josh. 'Now explain why we have to have Karl along.'

Karl flicked a warning glance at Josh.

Josh winced. 'Cos I'm only a second year and I can't practice without a licensed practitioner in the neighborhood. Since Karl passed Year five, he has a license.'

Karl tucked up his knees and sat crossed legged on the back seat. Josh slid into the front. Penny started the engine. 'Okay, where do we go now?'

Karl leaned forwards. 'Tell me how you lost Mr. Trewithick.'

Josh glanced at Penny to check she wasn't going to reply, but she just reversed the car. 'He took Philip off to talk about that fire, and when I tried to contact him half an hour ago, his phone was switched off.'

Karl contorted his body and pulled out his own phone. He tapped a couple of buttons and held it to his ear. He grimaced, and touched another button. 'Philip's phone is offline too. Please go to the vicarage, Penny.'

Penny turned right.

'But we need to look at that house,' Josh said. 'It's got this curse dripping down the walls. And--'

Karl held up a hand. 'We need to see if we can trace Trewithick. I'll guide you through a location working, but that's easiest with either something belonging to the person or at the last place you saw them.'

'And why can't you do it?' demanded Penny.

Karl sighed. 'I've been transferred to Trewithick because I can only do defense. Josh is good at attack, I've seen him scrapping in Antique Gym, but I reckon he sleeps through morning service so doesn't know as much of the prayer book as he should.' He grinned at Josh, who smiled ruefully.

'I don't know why you're so het up about his disappearance,' said Penny, pulling up outside the vicarage. 'He's a full-grown witchfinder. He can keep himself safe, better than either of you can.'

Josh traded a look with Karl and said, 'Mr. Trewithick's not been ... well, recently.'

'He's past the normal retirement age for our career,' added Karl.

Getting out, Josh pulled up the seat to let Karl unfold from the back seat. 'You should go for a bigger car, Pen. Right Josh, let's...' He stopped as Penny got out of the car. 'You'd be better off staying out of this, Penny.'

'If Philip's in trouble, I need to help.' She hitched her handbag over her shoulder in a decisive manner.

Karl looked at the staff in his hands then back up at his sister. 'If you promise to run and not get into a fight.'

Penny stared right back at him. She looked first away, but made no promises.

Josh fished in his pocket. 'I'll get Mr. Trewithick's sword. I can use it as the personal item and use it's good for defense too.'

'Does it feed you?' Karl fell into step beside him.

'Yes, it links me to the Universe. I feel invincible.'

'Take care that you don't start believing that.'

'Not likely to. Having Mr. Dunkley haul me out of one mess is enough.'

'He can be scathing,' said Karl. He looked over his shoulder. 'Pen, if you're coming come, but remember, don't get into a fight.'

Josh heard Penny's shoes clicking on the paving slabs as they reached Mr. Trewithick's van. 'I last spoke to him in the churchyard,' he said, after taking the sword and re-locking the van.

Even sheathed he could feel the sword singing to the dark matter in the Universe. He hugged the sword to his chest as the song stroked his bones.

'Where were you?' asked Karl.

'Here.' Josh led the way to the puddle and drew the sword. The butterflies flew around him in chaotic frenzy, caught in the song-lines of the sword. The shifting colors tugged at his Sight.

The moorland under paw, the moon lighting the hunting trail. The flash of a silver blade in the rising sun. The hatred and despair.

Josh gritted his teeth. Mr. Trewithick: he tried to draw the image of his Master in his mind.

Bitter pain: damn her for doing this to me. A circle in the front room, huddled until dawn.

Golden hair, graying now, shocking blue eyes that see the soul. Mr. Trewithick, I need to find him. The flashing colors pulled his eyes upward to the circling sky. Clouds painted on the purest blue, reflected in lifted the sword.

Through the blue and into the darkness, it's cold here. Not even the sun can warm into the cold places of stone. Then Joy, purest pain of happiness, a child's cry.

Pain.

'What's happening?' That voice was female.

'He's gone too deep.' A man's voice. His face was slapped again. 'Josh! Open your mouth.'

Something was held to his lips. Liquid sunshine poured into his mouth. He swallowed, the fire warmed the cold stone that was his innermost self. Brandy.

'Stone, he's on stone. The paws, the moon,' Josh said, when he got his mouth under control again. He focused on Karl who had him resting on his shoulder.

'Come all the way back, Josh.'

'There was a baby...' Josh shook his head. 'It's gone. But none of it was now. Some of what I saw was forged into the sword from his past and some floated on the storm winds from what may happen.'

'For God's sake Josh, next time wait until the words can focus you,' muttered Karl.

The church gate squealed open. 'What are you doing here?'

Karl caught up his staff and he stood. 'We are Investigative Officers of the Church. State your business.'

'That's Mr. Willoughby, the vicar. He used to be my RE teacher.' Josh held himself upright on his elbow. 'Did you see where Mr. Trewithick went after I left to chase fairies?'

'When I left, your Mr. Trewithick was here talking to all of you.'

'Thank you,' said Karl and turned back to where Josh was struggling to his feet.

'No wait, Mr. Willoughby can help us.'

'I beg your pardon?' said Willoughby. 'Why would I want to do that?'

Josh staggered over to Karl and leaned on him. 'Because you know that prayer book off by heart. Karl will work the protections and I can work the attack, but I need you to feed me the lines.'

Willoughby shook his head. 'If you had listened in my class you wouldn't be failing now.' He sounded smug. 'In my day they didn't let just anyone into the Investigative Office.'

'And they didn't let you,' said Penny. 'It takes a lot of courage to make a witchfinder. It's easier to instill the knowledge than it is to teach courage.'

Willoughby snorted. Both Karl and Josh glared at Penny.

'It's true,' she said.

'Shut up,' said Josh. He turned away from her. 'Mr. Willoughby, I need your help. Please.'

'No!' He turned on his heel and strode towards the gate.

Karl shook his head. 'I didn't want to do this, but you know the Laws.'

Willoughby stopped dead. 'Don't you dare, young man.'

Karl reached to this inside pocket and brought out his wallet. He flipped it open and produced the shiny new license. 'The Laws state that all reasonable help requested by an Investigative Officer must be rendered. I request, in the name of the Church, your aid in this matter.'

Josh suddenly remembered what had bothered him back at the house. 'Why were those girls carrying teen dolls?' He turned to Penny. 'Teenagers don't play with dolls do they?'

Willoughby looked down his nose at the gathering.

'Some might,' said Penny, doubtfully.

'Where are you going with this thought?' asked Karl.

'We need to get back to your friend's house.' Josh spun and looked at Willoughby. 'I'm sorry I was a pest in your class Mr. Willoughby, but I need your help now. Could you get your Book of Common Prayer and join us?'

'I am required to,' said Willoughby.

'Oh God!' said Josh. 'He'll be no use. Release him Karl, I'll get a copy of the prayer book from the van and hope I can flick through it and get what I need in time.' Bracing himself, Josh sheathed the sword.

Willoughby stood in his path. He pulled a prayer book from his pocket and brandished it at Josh. 'I said I'd do it. You won't dismiss me that easily. You'll see that I was right.'

Josh shut away his anger. 'Let's get going. Mr. Willoughby with me.'

'Come on, Penny.' Karl grabbed Penny's arm and led the way out of the churchyard.

Once at the van, Josh slammed into the driving seat. 'Right, what I need are simple words to help me focus the energies I'm calling down. They've got to be relevant. I'll say things like fire or wind. Can you manage that?'

Willoughby flicked through the black leather bound volume as Josh drove through the late afternoon traffic. He pulled up behind the red sports car. Karl stood watching the house.

'Should he be standing in the open like that?' said Willoughby.

Josh smiled. 'No one can see him, unless he wants them to.'

Karl walked towards them, his expression set in marble. He nodded at Josh, who climbed out of Trewithick's van, still carrying the sword.

As Karl held the miasma of the house at bay, Josh put his hands up to face and took three deep breaths. He felt the calm of a working slip over his mind and lowered his hands. Willoughby stared at him.

Through the calm, Josh said, 'Stick near me. I can protect you that way.' He tapped the sword.

Josh saw what he had missed before. Under the vortex of power and pain circling the house was gleeful delight. The curse was a cover set by the owners as a way of sidetracking people like himself. The vortex spiraled down into the back garden.

Karl balanced the staff over both hands, then nodded. He dropped the staff to one hand and led the way. Both Penny and Willoughby followed behind Josh and Karl as they paraded down the drive and circled the house.

Karl stopped, still hidden by the corner of the house, and planted the staff. He gestured Josh forward.

What caught Josh's eye was not the gaggle of girls in front of the pond, set between a shed and a rockery, but the gaudily-painted garden gnome fishing from a rock.

He winced, then gazed warily at the pond. He hated ponds, you never knew what lurked in the bottom of them. Dragonflies hovered serenely over the water, and butterflies glided through the garden.

'There's right powerful restraining spells all over that shed,' he muttered to Karl.

But Penny answered. 'It would have to be to hold a powerful practitioner like Mr. Trewithick. What's happening over there?'

Josh scanned over the layers of protection that smothered the garden and on towards the girls.

He let his hearing focus on the girls.

'By this link,' intoned one teenager at two girls covered in butterflies. 'Let the doll take the fat, let the girl remain forever slender.'

One of the girls fell to the ground, startling the butterflies into flight. She lay there shuddering.

With his odd sight, Josh could see what was happening. Far too much of the girl's spirit strength was leaking down a link into one of the four plastic teen dolls that lay on the ground. The dolls didn't look right. Instead of the impossibly thin waist and immaculate breasts, these dolls were dumpy. Feeling it with his sight, he could sense each doll was tied to a person present. Was it a voodoo doll? It had sort of reverse feel to it.

It had to stop.

Dropping the sheath to the ground, he charged to the rescue, skipping over the under layers of warning lines. Wielding the soul sword he chopped through the teen doll. The link snapped; the girl's soul light jumped back into her body and she lay panting.

'I warned you to eat before the ceremony,' shouted the leader. 'And who are you?' She took a breath. 'DAD!'

Josh looked at her in disbelief at her callous behavior. Now what was he supposed to do? Attack the girls? He turned to get advice from Karl.

Just in time to see Willoughby step straight through the first alert line.

Josh held up a hand 'No! Stay there!'

Over by the pond the dragonflies formed an attack squadron. Josh charged in front of Willoughby. Butterflies flew straight into his eyes, dragonflies buzzed past him. He swung the sword at them, but it was like swatting flies with a chopstick.

Josh called the song of the wind. It howled around the chimney pot and spun into the garden. He dropped to the ground as the elemental curled and danced around its playthings, sucking the flying army into a vortex.

He crawled to where Mr. Willoughby huddled on the ground.

'You okay?'

Mr Willoughby raised a hand and inspected it. 'They burnt me.'

'Sorry,' said Josh. 'I told you to stay beside me, then forgot to tell you to stay back.'

'You rushed back to help me,' said Willoughby. 'Even though you hate me.'

Josh grinned. 'No point in training to be a professional hero, if you have any sense of self-preservation.'

'DAD!' screamed the girl again.

Josh spun to call in his back up and saw Penny had snuck round to the shed. She tugged at the hasp of the brass padlock then her hand plunged into her handbag. Shaking his head, he ignored her priorities. 'Karl, bring the wards closer. Willoughby, with me.'

Karl stepped into the garden proper. From a great distance he spoke. 'Stop using random power, Josh. It's too uncontrolled; you will hurt someone. Controlled usage, that's why you have Willoughby with you.'

Josh reined in the sword. He knew what Karl said was true, but he wanted to feel the song of the sword in his bones. He turned to Willoughby. 'Still got your book?'

Willoughby nodded and thumbed through the tissue paper pages barely looking at the words.

'Josh!' Karl shouted.

Josh looked around and saw the patio door opening. Breathing heavily as he tried to control the sense of Ultimate Unity with the Universe, he swung the sword around.

The door slid open and a man, dressed in jeans and a tee shirt walked out. 'Now what's going on Jessica? What do you think you're doing?' He strode towards the interrupted ceremony.

'But Dad--'

'Don't tell me you're doing that silly slimming spell again? I warned when you put Chloë in hospital--'

Jessica pointed at the gathering.

The man saw Penny. 'Stop!' He ran out onto the lawn. 'Don't open that door!'

Glancing over his shoulder, Josh saw Penny was crouched, unscrewing the bottom hinge of the shed door. The top hinge flapped loose. He sidestepped and stood in front of the man, lifting the blade slightly.

'I need words for a holding,' Josh said.

Willoughby fluttered through the pages.

'Stop her!' shouted the man. 'That door mustn't be opened.' He and Josh pranced about in a pushing blocking dance.

Finally, he pleaded with Josh. 'Don't let it out!'

It, the man had said, not him or them. Josh spun around to see Penny pull the door out of the frame.

Bindings shattered in the crystalline air. A stream of Darkness howled out of the shed, flattening Penny. The acrid stench of stale weedkiller, mixed with wet rot and turpentine, washed over the garden. The essence of the Darkness clawed at Josh's mind, blinding his Sight.

'Josh!' shouted Karl.

Josh gawped at the pale, imitation reality. It was a cardboard cut out world. He'd forgotten what the world looked like without seeing the Life in everything--if he had ever seen anything that way.

A knot of despair worked its way up from his gut. He couldn't smell the sky. His body felt only the clothes encasing it. No windsong stirred the marrow of his bones.

He had been gelded.

'Josh!'

Jessica grabbed her friend who had collapsed and pulled her away from the pond. The other two stood staring at the horrific Darkness, until Jessica kicked them.

He couldn't hear the words she said, not with his special senses gone, but they each grabbed an arm and helped tug their friend away. They huddled against the shed, in glassy-eyed terror.

'JOSH!'

The desperate note in Karl's voice re-called him and he turned, dazed, to face Karl. He could see the sweat trickling down Karl's temple.

'Do something Josh! I can't hold the wards.'

Shock jolted Josh. Karl could hold against *anything*. He looked around and saw the darkness congealing onto the garden gnome. The acid life of the Darkness ate at the gaudy paint.

Do something? What could he do without his Sight?

Butterflies and dragonflies swarmed in a gleeful ballet around the Creature.

He could channel the strength like all the officers of the Church, except he hadn't paid attention to the words, because he never needed to. He looked around. Willoughby knelt on the ground near Penny, praying. Penny was tucked into a ball, rocking on her knees.

Josh scrambled to his feet and charged across the lawn. He grabbed Willoughby by the collar and shook him.

'Get me some words, prayer boy!' Josh retrieved the Book of Common Prayer and stuffed it into Willoughby's hand.

Karl dropped to his knees, still just holding the wards.

Josh turned back to Willoughby, who held the book as if he'd never seen a prayer before. Penny uncurled. She grabbed the prayer book and flipped open a page. In terror she glanced over the pond at the creature then back to the page.

'Words,' begged Josh. When this was over he swore he would memorize every last bloody word in the prayer book.

The last of the paint crackled away, and the Darkness sank, slowly, into the concrete gnome.

A sharp crack, and another. Penny and Josh both looked up from the prayer book. The gnome crumbled. By the shed Jessica crumpled against her friends. One of them patted her face, uncertainly.

The butterflies circled, trapped by Karl's wards.

'Of course--butterflies--it's an air elemental,' shouted Josh. 'Earth words and binding the winds.'

Penny nodded and turned another page.

'Bring them into the pit of destruction,' Penny shouted, her finger on the page.

Josh stood. He lifted his hand and summoned the Strength as he had been taught, visualized an outcome and spoke. '*Bring them into the pit of destruction.*' His voice cracked, like he was a teenager again.

From the dust that used to be the gnome, a vortex of pain and power rose above the pond.

Josh could feel the strength flowing from him, in a way he'd never felt before.

Beside him Penny skimmed through the pages of the Prayer Book. The vortex slowed as the ground split and sucked at the Creature. Then the swirling sped up. The creature lifted the spike of its Vortex free from the ground.

'Become as dung on the ground,' shouted Penny over the wind wuthering around the chimney pots.

Josh bent over as the wind sucked breath from his lungs. Straightening, he saw Penny rummaging in her bag. She tossed him a packet of glucose tablets. He fielded it and stuffed two in his mouth.

He visualized the creature touching the ground again. '*Become as dung on the ground!*'

Again he felt his life falling out of his skin as he pulled at the Creature. Waves scuttered over the pond as the wind whipped them into life, releasing the stench of rotting pondweed. And all around the Creature, insects of the air danced in anticipation.

The head of the vortex bowed towards them. Fighting the pull of the wind on his body, Josh stepped in front of Penny and Willoughby.

'*Become as dung on the ground!*' he shouted again. He took another step forward. He had to guard the civilians.

A hand touched his shoulder. Then Willoughby shouted in his ear. 'Thy storms do vex me, thou dost rule the storms of the sea.'

Gathering the last of his strength, Josh shouted. '*Thy storms do vex me, Thou dost rule the Storms of the Sea.*'

Below the creature, the pond stilled, and the gagging stink faded. The Creature twirled more slowly.

'Into the pit He digs for the ungodly,' quoted Willoughby.

Coughing at the draw on his lungs, Josh stammered out, '*Into the pit He digs for the ungodly.*'

The head of the Creature bowed away from him.

Josh held the image in his mind. The edges of the sky were turning black.

He must not pass out. He felt something at his lips, when he opened it he found another glucose tablet slipped into his mouth by Willoughby.

From the corner of his eye he saw Penny run over to Karl, penknife ready. Flicking horrified glances at the creature she cut across her fingers, then bracing herself, she cut Karl's hand.

'*Blood to blood, take my strength,*' she said.

The shock jolted Josh. The college was adamant that women were unable to control the strength like the college trained, but Penny was clearly conversant.

Karl lifted his head, eyes focused on his invisible wards. The pit hauled at the creature, but Josh felt his strength leaking away.

He heard feet pounding on the path by the house. Just what they needed, more family to fight.

'*Into the pit He digs for the ungodly.*' shouted Trewithick.

'A raise in the air pressure,' shouted a second voice.

And Josh felt the drain of his life force ease. He collapsed onto his hands, not knowing when he had dropped to his knees.

'Josh!' shouted Penny.

Almost sighing, Josh looked up. The man of the house was running toward Mr. Trewithick's sword. Pushing up on his hands, Josh made a racing start for the sword. The man got there first. With gleeful madness in his eyes, he clenched his hand around the pommel.

Josh ploughed straight into him, knocking him flat. Pinning him down, Josh pounded on the man's wrist, until he heard the man scream-- the squeal of a pig in anguish.

Pain and fear warred for dominance on the man's face. With his free hand he attempted to prise his fingers open.

Josh laid his hand over the man's and spoke the only words he remembered. '*And they were brought down in their wickedness.*'

The man stared at Josh, then his eyes rolled back in his head as he lay still.

A whisper of power sang to Josh from the sword and his weariness dropped away. Faint color leached back into the world, though nothing became as clear as usual.

Cautiously standing, he *Saw* Mr. Trewithick: a figure of pure, golden fire. But deep inside the fire was a cold, black coal. Beside Trewithick was Philip Stempress with the same dusky soulfire as Karl.

Intrigued, Josh stalked towards his mentor.

Trewithick raised his eyes, and Josh saw fear. The Creature was dropping oh-so-slowly into the pit and the black coal inside Trewithick was growing--sending tendrils through Mr. Trewithick's soul.

To one side Josh saw Karl failing again.

'Do something, Josh.' Penny still clung to Karl, trying to feed him her spirit fire.

Distracted from his mentor, Josh looked for anything he could do. He squinted, trying to focus his wavering Sight.

The Creature was drawing power from the people present. He *saw* the lines running between them, but the power all ran one way.

The two biggest sources of the Creature's strength were the man of the house and his daughter, Jessica. Both unconscious, they were unable to resist the draw.

He had a sword in his hand. Walking over to the man he lifted the blade in both hands to stab down.

Penny's mouth dropped open, her eyes wide in horror.

He stopped. That was murder. Could he just cut the line?

He started to gather the power of the sword.

'No!' Josh almost sang. 'That's the easy way.' He clawed at his inner self and found the strength he needed. He slashed at the air and the line snapped.

His arms and legs felt shivery with relief. He staggered over to Jessica, and did the same motion. She blinked and sat up.

Looking up he saw Trewithick standing tall. 'Karl!' Trewithick said. 'Bring your wards in. Josh, cut the other links.'

Jessica and the other three girls cowered against the shed. Their links were intertwined.

'No! We didn't mean anything wrong! We only wanted to be thin,' whispered Jessica. 'Don't kill us.'

Josh ignored her as he sliced through the links to the Creature.

Then he shivered as Karl's wards passed through him.

Closer and closer they moved to the Creature, which now howled in terror.

He turned to walk away from the girls, when he saw the other links, the ones that went to the dolls. These girls had caused all this trouble; they deserved punishment. He sliced through the links to the dolls.

'NO!' Jessica wailed. The waxy pallor to their skin faded and the full breasts shrank to normal size. Josh turned his gaze away as the skinny jeans ripped. He walked back to the fight.

Mr. Trewithick held up his swordstick. *'At Thy rebuke, they flee: Thou hast set their bounds on them that they may not pass!'*

The creature clawed at the air. Dust swirled up around it and reformed the fishing gnome. Karl's wards sank into the statue repainting it in gaudy colors.

And the garden was calm.

Trewithick stalked to the garden gnome and tucked it under his arm, then he spun around, his eyes blazing with all the strength he had just used to encapsulate the demon. 'What the Hell do you lot think you were playing at here? Engaging a demon without me?'

Josh laid the sword on the ground. He tucked his hands behind him and looked down. 'But your phone was turned off, Sir. We... I thought you'd been taken, so I ran for Karl.'

'At least you had some sense! Of course I turned my phone off. I went into the Church to chat with Philip. Your training in Religious Manners is severely wanting.' He cast a fulminating glance at where Willoughby knelt gazing at Josh. Then the eyes on fire turned to Karl. 'Well?'

'I heard that you were with Philip, and checked Philip's phone, which was also off. I don't have any excuse, Sir.' Karl smiled ruefully. 'But I will say this, Josh is a natural team leader.'

Trewithick took a deep breath, and the fire in his spirit faded. The marble statue melted into a man. 'Well, there's no harm done.' He turned to Philip. 'Unconventional methods, but thank you for joining in.'

Philip turned his back on them. Penny took a hesitant step towards Philip, until Karl waved her back.

To the side, Philip looked back at Trewithick uncertainly. Trewithick held out his left hand.

Philip strode over to Trewithick and took the hand. He dropped to one knee before Trewithick, who placed his right hand on Philip's bowed head. Josh saw the tears on Philip's face.

Penny fisted her hands. 'Why can't women train at your stupid college? I hate you all.' She stormed out of the garden.

Trewithick smiled sadly then looked around. 'We'd better get this mess cleaned up.'

Yes, thought Josh, *why don't they train girls at the college?* He glanced around and saw the prayer book on the ground. He picked it up and brushed off the grass stains. 'Here's your book, Mr. Willoughby. Thanks for the help.'

Willoughby still knelt in the muddy grass.

'I didn't fail with you.' Willoughby shook his head. 'But I failed you. I couldn't have done what you did!'

Josh shrugged, uncomfortable with Willoughby's praise. 'Hey! We can't all be stupid enough to be professional heroes.'

Willoughby curled Josh's fingers around the book. 'Take it, it's yours.' Then with a touch of his previous asperity he added, 'And this time, boy, learn it.'

Served Cold

Josh lobbed another chip over the seawall. Seagulls instantly dive-bombed it, shrieking their defiance of their rivals. Then they mobbed the victor, trying to steal the scraps.

'I have every confidence in you.' A man talking on his mobile broke walked through the gulls' scrum and they scattered, leaving behind a mess of cold potato. 'Oh sure. I'd not miss that...Best served cold an' all.'

For once this summer, it wasn't raining. There was even a bit of sun. Some of the more adventurous holidaymakers had shed their coats and walked about letting the sun onto skin that looked more like it was the end of winter than the middle of summer.

He sat on the low beach wall and let the waves roll in--at least watching the people was better than carting the golfing bags around for Mr. Dunkley and Mr. Trewithick. Sometimes he even saw people using Cræft. A lot of people just did instinctive stuff and he liked to watch and learn.

Today, for instance, that man who chased off the gulls was doing something with his mobile, besides talking into it. It took Josh a moment to notice the man was consciously controlling the strength he was directing. The lines of power circled a little, this close to the sea, but Josh was interested to note that the salty water was providing a kind of shielding to the working. If he hadn't been sitting so close he would never have observed the spell.

'Dave!'

Josh looked up at the shout. A man, in biking leathers and wearing his soft-brow hair in the trademark college ponytail, dashed across the road.

The man stuffed his mobile away. 'Mike! What are you doing here?'

'Business,' Mike said. 'I would have thought you'd be at Gail's side. What with her being in labor and all.'

'You're not getting me with that,' said Dave. 'It's too early.'

Curious, Josh watched as Mike slotted a working into place around them, so that no one would see the argument. Again, the salty water made it difficult to follow the intricate tracery of the power lines. This Mike knew what he was doing too. Wondering if he should help, Josh saw that nothing Dave tried was sticking to Mike. And which one should he be helping?

'Yeah!' Mike said. 'Far too early!' He grabbed Dave by the shoulders ramming his knees against the beach wall.

'Back off Mike,' said Dave. 'You'll have me over into the sea, and then where would Gail be?'

'Better off without her bastard husband,' Mike shouted into his face. He caught Dave in an arm lock. 'I'm going to see you get onto a train to York.'

Dave tried to wriggle free, then tried forcing Mike away with a working.

'Gosh Dave!' Mike said. 'You've gone all flabby since you flunked out of the fifth year.'

Mike prepared to strong-arm Dave off the sea front.

'Look Mike,' said Dave. 'If you're going to send me packing at least let me use my car.'

'Na-uh! Especially as I know you have laid some ritual-strong counter charms on it. I saw that at Christmas. You're going to get on the first train going in the right direction.' Mike leant in to whisper but Josh was close enough to hear. 'If I even suspect you're cheating on my sister, you're for the high jump.'

Josh jumped up and crammed the chip wrapper in the nearby bin. 'Mr... Ummm, Sir? Should you be doing that?'

Mike darted a glance over at Josh then, seeing Josh's red hair tied in a college ponytail, he relaxed.

'That's right,' said Dave. 'You shouldn't be using your training on random family disagreements.'

Mike slipped his hand into Dave's pocket and brought out the mobile phone. He tossed it to Josh. 'Dump that in the sea will you, please.' He turned back to Dave. 'I know you and Dunkley worked out a lot of tricks with technology.'

'You think your Dunkley is so full of rectitude,' Dave said as Josh fielded the phone left-handed. 'But I learnt from him. Have you ever looked at his dogs?'

Hefting the mobile Josh mouthed, 'Really?' at Mike.

Mike nodded, his lips fixed into a fierce grin.

Carefully shielding his actions from the people around them by drawing in the sun and the salt air as camouflage, Josh lobbed the mobile into the in-coming tide. He wished he'd been allowed to examine it; he wanted to unravel the workings Dave had been using.

Mike gritted his teeth, then sent sprawling Dave to the pavement. Cold potato smeared over his fancy business suit.

'Get back to Gail,' Mike said. The shifty sea air left Josh unsure as to whether Mike had added a twist to his working.

As Dave scrambled to his feet and stalked away, Mike turned to Josh. 'And you don't interfere again. You might end up splatted between a duel.'

'No, Sir!'

'Only the older ones insist on that formality, I'm Mike, Mike Rider,' he said. 'You are?'

'Josh Analay.'

Mike stared through the thin crowd at Dave's retreating back. 'Mr. Trewithick's new apprentice? I thought I'd be the last, but he's still refusing to retire, isn't he? Right, I've got him going home.'

'I take it that's someone you don't like,' Josh said. 'How d'you know he'll go home?'

Mike chuckled. 'I set a working on him that I knew he couldn't have the knowledge to break, based on the Deeper Mysteries--you learn those after year five.'

Josh looked away from the seagulls. 'You mean he was one of us?'

'Yeah, once. Dave Green, he flunked year five.' Suddenly Mike's face went all glassy. 'Green! There's green everywhere!'

Josh's mouth dropped open. All Mike's shielding dropped away as his strength became locked up in his Sight.

Darting a glance around, Josh saw people beginning to notice Mike. He caught Mike by the arm as he to babble about lightning crawling up the walls and called the sun and the salt air around them. The holidaymakers looked away.

Josh tugged on Mike until he started walking.

'There's a flame, an ancient statue of my girlfriend,' Mike said.

Josh was trying to remember what Mike said while leading him to a bench--it was difficult with Mike being so engrossed in his Vision. He'd never had to keep his mind on so much at once, but he kept everyone looking away.

Mike looked at him earnestly. 'The men are ashamed and hiding, and the sand is so shifty.'

'Flames, statues, green, lightning,' Josh muttered.

'Danger, death and fire. The buffet is served cold. At threes'

Then all six-foot of Mike folded up.

Josh managed to deflect him onto the bench, and kept his head from hitting anything, but there were going to be bruises. He patted the pockets of Mike's leather biking jacket and found a packet of glucose tablets. Mike blinked, then raised a hand to rub his eyes.

'Here take this.' Josh held a sweet to Mike's mouth.

It opened like a baby bird and Josh dropped the sweet in.

Still without opening his eyes, Mike groaned. 'I hate the Sight. It knocks me flat.'

'Would golf have anything to do with your warning,' Josh asked. 'I mean, you talked about greens.'

Mike's eyes flicked open. 'Yes! Golf that's part of the green, but Dave Green is there too. Where are Dunkley and Trewithick? They're in danger!'

Josh pressed him back against the bench. 'They're on the golf course. S'why I asked.'

'We've got to go and warn them. Dave would love to be revenged on Dunkley.' Mike pushed Josh away and staggered a few paces. He got his balance and started to sprint.

'Stop!' Josh shouted.

Mike slowed. 'We've got to warn them.'

'We've got to think how this Dave works,' Josh said catching up. 'He was talking to someone on the phone, about this. He intended to watch I think, but he's not done the setting up.'

Mike stopped. 'That's right. Dave wouldn't put his fingerprints on anything that could be traced to him. So who's he working with?'

'You said something about an old flame, perhaps an ex-girlfriend? And what about the men hiding shameful things?'

'The last one's easy,' Mike said. 'Dave's always said that Dunkley did bad stuff and hid it from the rest of us. No one believes it.'

Josh shrugged. 'How did he work? Did he like ritual or impulse?'

'For a second year you've got some truly deep insights here. He liked rituals, but if someone else...'

'Golf, ritual.' Josh waved a hand for silence then dug it into his hair. 'It'll be at the ninth hole.'

Josh turned to run, but Mike grabbed him. 'Tell me what you're talking about.'

Josh wondered if Mike were thick. 'The trap is set at the ninth hole.'

'Why?'

'Ritual of threes.'

'Why not the eighteenth?'

'If it were three times three times three then that's twenty seven-- there aren't 27 holes so it has to three plus three plus three and that's nine. Let's go.' Josh shook off Mike and started running, and shouted over his shoulder. 'We can start looking at the ninth, OK?'

Mike caught him easily as they ran through town. It took five minutes of steady jogging to reach the gate of the golf course. And then up the long drive.

Panting, Josh skidded to a halt beside the map posted on the clubhouse wall. None of the posh golfers took even a first look at them in scrappy jeans and biking leathers.

Josh traced a route to the ninth hole on map. Mike joined him, then his eyes defocused. Josh recognized it as dropping back into a vision.

Quickly he tugged the essence of wood and concrete from the clubhouse around them both and reached out to lead Mike to the nearest bench. Two men who had been resting there suddenly stood and went about their business still talking. But as Josh touched Mike, Mike blinked.

'You're right. It's the ninth hole,' he said and swayed slightly.

Josh reached into Mike's coat pocket and slipped out the packet of glucose tablets again and held them out to Mike as he led the man to the bench.

'How do you do this Sight stuff?' Josh asked. He had to call Mike out of this visionary state.

Mike mouthed another tablet. 'Why?' His voice was slurred.

'Because I didn't see any strength as they call it,' Josh said. 'Usually it's flying around. More so with gifted Cræft than our inherent usage, but it's still there.'

'What do you mean by that?' Mike asked. He turned to look at Josh, interest beginning to snap him out.

Josh shrugged. 'I can sort of see this strength it sort swirls around then slots into place when directed.'

'A sort of Sight?'

'Well that too, but it's like smell too. I can see it happening then the flavor of it lingers in the air like a smell.'

Mike lifted his eyebrows in respect. 'You're one of those are you. They're very rare, but I'd keep quiet about it outside of college. The gifted call your ability witch sniffing. It's not popular.' Mike sat up and took another sweet. 'I'll be fine now. Get up there and warn them--especially about Dave Green. I'll catch you up.'

Josh sprinted away in the direction he had gathered from the map. If his mission hadn't been so urgent, running over the cut lawns of the golf course would almost be a pleasure. The springy grass absorbed the impact of every step--much better than the concrete he usually had to pound his boots over while monster chasing. The sun beat down on him until he wished he had a hat, then he remembered what he was training to be and gathered a sea breeze to cool his run.

Off the smooth and into the rough, the grass and wild flowers lashed at his knees as he half ran, half skipped like a gazelle. He swatted ineffectually at the bees and flies swarming up around his head. He had to get to hole nine.

Then he could see it: a coil of darkness feeding into the ritual of the golf course.

It wasn't inherent Cræft, this strength was gifted from a demon, fed on hatred.

He skidded down a man-made hill in time to see a golf ball land in the sand bunker that was the center of the vortex. He tried to up his pace on the slippery grass but tripped and fell flat on his face. Spitting out his mouthful of cornflowers he saw Trewithick run towards the bunker.

'No! Sir!' Josh shouted.

Trewithick said something over his shoulder to someone out of sight. Then laughing he dropped onto the sand.

Scrambling to his feet Josh tried to wave Mr. Trewithick out of the pit. Trewithick concentrated on his sand-locked ball.

Josh charged on.

Mr. Dunkley came into sight and was about to join Trewithick in the sand.

Josh cupped his hands around his mouth. 'NO!'

Dunkley looked up and saw Josh. He stopped, then he turned and gestured Trewithick out of the bunker.

Just as the sun-baked sand rose up in a frantic dust devil around Trewithick.

Josh watched Dunkley drop his golf bag. He lifted his arms and shouted something into the dizzy spin of sand.

The sand fell away, revealing a figure made from twisting, living flame: a dragon fanned its fiery wings to raise the dusty screen.

At its feet Trewithick curled in a fetal position, head tucked into his arms.

Josh's mouth dropped open as he stared at the first major elemental he had encountered in his training. It towered over Dunkley.

A hand clamped over Josh's shoulder. He spun, hitting out. But Mike ducked away easily.

'Good work,' Mike said. He scanned the battleground.

'But I didn't get here in time to warn them.'

'You must have managed something,' Mike said. 'Else why isn't Dunkley caught in the trap too? Now let's see what we can do to help.'

'Oh right! What can a second year do?' Josh had quit trying to edge away, Mike's hand on his shoulder was rock solid.

'Tell me where the person controlling the fire elemental is,' Mike demanded

'What?'

'You said you can smell out power, well there should be a link between the dragon figure and the person misusing their Cræft.'

Josh glanced back at the fight. Dunkley was using his golf club as a single stick, beating away any flaming appendage that got too close. The two dogs barked and snapped on either side of the dragon, close enough to be a distraction, not close enough to get burnt. Equally Josh could see the calm workings of Water and Earth that Dunkley was using to try and dowse the fire.

Trewithick began to uncurl from the center of the bunker. He saw what was happening and painfully levered himself onto hands and knees to crawl across the sand away from the fight.

'Well?' asked Mike.

'The fire elemental, the initial trap spell spinning loose and all that stuff Dunkley's chucking around so casually are blocking anything else.'

Mike sighed. 'They won't be in the middle of all that mess--like a general they will be watching from the sidelines. Widen your viewpoint.'

Josh took some deep breaths. The flaring of everything going on in the bunker was giving him a headache to look at. Rubbing his temples he let the corner of his eye do the looking for him. He often found that worked better than staring straight at something.

Nothing.

Then he saw a line of puss-green hatred leading from the dragon towards a water trap.

'It's going to the lake.'

'Thanks Josh. Come on, keep me on track but don't get in the way. But I can see you're more sensible than ever I was about that.' Mike grinned at Josh. 'But it doesn't do to be too cautious in this job.'

With that sort of encouragement Josh tagged along after Mike. *What I should be doing*, he thought, *is getting out of here.*

Out loud he said, 'The track leads this way.'

Mike slowed. 'Can you tell how close we are?' he whispered.

Josh frowned. Behind him the din was drowning out the minor scent. He shook his head.

Mike nodded then dropped so that he could crawl to see over the brow of the hill.

Josh copied him. On the other side, they saw a woman standing peering into what looked like a plasma globe.

'Bloody hell,' whispered Mike. 'I know her. We shut down her health spa for older men. She had this special brew that increased their flagging libidos.'

'Is she an ex-girlfriend?' Josh asked.

Mike flushed as he glanced over at Josh. 'No. Ummm. Have you ever met a succubus?'

Josh shook his head, eyes alight with interest.

'Well they show you a person you love. She had a fire elemental before too, and I saw an old girl friend, that's all.' He stood and shouted. *'The earth trembled and quaked, the very foundations of the hills shook and were removed.'*

A rolling wave of an earthquake knocked the woman off her feet.

She dropped the globe. The wave of earth grabbed the ball and pushed it towards the lake. The woman screamed in outrage and crawled over the shifting earth to retrieve her power.

Mike sprinted down the hill after his attack. *'The springs of waters were seen.'*

Josh watched, impressed as the earth split open and a fountain of water spurted up to cool the globe.

From behind him he heard a great hissing and the damp, dusty smell of wet road after a long dry spell wash over him.

Staying low to the ground, he ducked away from Mike's fight. He wanted to see what was happening with Trewithick and Dunkley.

He followed the strand of hatred back. The cord thickened and he flung himself at the ground shielding his eyes in his arms.

His odd Sight, that Mike called witch sniffing, had saved him as the fire elemental was hauled back along the line that linked it to the globe. It passed over his head and the heat pulled all the oxygen from the air. Gasping, he tried to crawl away, then it was gone. He lifted his head as air rushed into fill the void. The hot wind slapped him across his exposed hands. They felt sunburned.

Dunkley charged over the hill after the elemental, his dogs at his heels. Josh rolled out of his way, but Ross stopped and sniffed Josh on the ground and licked his face.

Josh sat up, scratching the dog's ear, while keeping a wary eye out for more danger.

Ross suddenly turned and growled. Trewithick, looking singed and dazed walked slowly behind.

'Ross!' Dunkley shouted and the dog sprinted after its master.

Trewithick stopped and looked at Josh as if wondering who he was then smiled.

'Come on son, what's happened over here?'

'Mike Rider took on the elemental's controller,' Josh said, getting to his feet. 'Are you all right sir? I tried to warn you, but I slipped.'

'No harm done, hey.' Trewithick rested a trembling hand on Josh's shoulder and Josh led the way over the hill.

Dunkley and Mike had the woman in handcuffs by the time they arrived. The globe was still sparking, even after the bath, singeing the grass where it lay.

Trewithick lifted his hand off Josh's shoulder and made his way towards the grouping. Josh trotted alongside, he didn't think that Trewithick was steady enough but realized that the man had his pride.

Ross and Rory both barked as Trewithick bent and picked up the globe with bare hands.

'Nathaniel, I don't think...' Dunkley said.

Trewithick turned with a distant smile on his face and unseeing eyes. His hands formed into claws to hold the dragon globe.

The captive smiled triumphantly as Trewithick lifted the globe above his head and looked vaguely at Mike.

'*For at his word the stormy winds arise which lifted up the waves,*' Trewithick said, so quietly that Josh was the only one who heard.

Waves like huge white claws surged up in the lake taking raking bites out of the shoreline. Time seemed to slow. The captive's triumphal smile faded into horror the wave was poised to drown her as well as the two men.

Josh saw lines of strength slotting into place. Dunkley and Mike shouted words lost in the roaring of the waves.

What can I do that they can't? I'm just a second year, Josh thought.

As the waves smashed at the barriers that Dunkley and Mike were trying to erect, Josh remembered that the lines that Trewithick used were from Morning Prayer; he also had the next bit memorized. A lot of the offensive workings were followed by very calming phrases.

What was Mike Rider's passing comment? Oh yes, *It doesn't do to be too cautious in this job.*

With the wave arching over to collapse on Dunkley and Mike, Josh shouted, '*For he makes the storms to cease and stills the waves.*'

The working shattered and pulled the wave back into the pond of the water trap. The surface calmly reflected cloudless sky.

The strength that Trewithick had used to perform the working, doubled by the additions from the fire elemental, grounded through Trewithick.

The globe dropped from Trewithick's nerveless fingers. His hands fisted in front of his chest. A soundless scream formed on his lips as he gasped for air.

The globe rolled to lie at Josh's feet. He gave it a flying kick into the lake.

A great hissing gasp of steam rose up and belched into the bright sky.

Dunkley dashed forward and caught Trewithick as he fell. His hand groped at Trewithick's neck.

Josh echoed Dunkley's sigh of relief.

'He's not dead.' Dunkley pulled out his mobile and punched a number with his thumb. While waiting for the call to be answered the tutor stared at Josh, thoughtfully. He looked away. 'Nathaniel Trewithick has collapsed on the course at the lake on the ninth hole. Do you think... Ah yes thank you.'

Mike knocked the woman to the ground and held her there. Leaning on the captive Mike asked Josh, 'How did you do that? How did you stop his working?'

'But it's...' Josh stopped. Behind Mike's back Dunkley held a finger to his lips--not a working but a request. 'I don't know,' Josh ended.

'Rider, lock our penitent in my car,' Dunkley said. He glanced at Josh, who remembered he had the keys.

He tossed them to Mike.

A Land Rover roared over the course and up to them. Two people in paramedic uniforms jumped out with cases and equipment and charged to Trewithick. They wasted no time in getting him on a stretcher and into the vehicle. They didn't notice that Mike had the woman pinned out in full view.

'Bastards,' she shouted, though the medics couldn't hear. 'You ruin my business, now this.'

'You were given a warning not to misuse your Cræft; you have ignored us,' Mike said. He jerked her to her feet and walked her away over the golf course.

Dunkley gave an order to his dogs in Scots Gaelic and they followed Mike.

'Joshua, you and I will pick up the golf bags.'

Swallowing hard, Josh followed Dunkley.

'How did you know how to do that?' Dunkley asked.

Josh shrugged. 'I'd noticed that a lot of the offensive workings were paired in the prayer book with calm responses, so it seemed worth trying.'

'Very well thought out. It's arranged that way to make it easier to deal with our people if they stray from the straight path. But as you can see it does have consequences.'

They retrieved the golf bags and walked back to the clubhouse in silence. Mike joined them at the door--alone.

'I've knocked her out,' he said. 'Your dogs are keeping watch.'

The manager of the course led them to a first aid room. The paramedic came up to them. 'He seems to have suffered a mild heart attack. He's stable now but we've summoned an ambulance.'

Dunkley waved a hand and the course officials left the four men alone.

Trewithick groaned as they entered. 'What happened?'

Mike looked between Trewithick and Josh. 'Josh put the brake on the working you were being compelled to perform on us.'

Trewithick lifted his head and stared at Josh. 'You shouldn't have been able to do that!'

Dunkley stepped into Trewithick's view. 'Nathaniel, I'm impressed. I knew you were a good teacher, but training a second year to able to intuit the deep mysteries... I think we'll need to transfer him to my tutelage now.'

Trewithick looked away from his friend to his hands. Bruises were beginning to form from where they had transformed. There were blisters on the tips. 'I...' He stopped and took a breath. 'Yes, he's yours.'

Dunkley indicated, with flicked finger, that Josh and Mike should move aside. Mike grabbed Josh and led him to look out of the window.

Mike watched Trewithick and Dunkley for a moment then turned away. Josh couldn't stop staring in horror as Dunkley crouched down to talk to ashen-faced Trewithick.

'What have I done?' whispered Josh.

The ambulance siren howling up the drive towards the clubhouse drowned out his words.

www.ingramcontent.com/pod-product-compliance
Lightning Source LLC
Chambersburg PA
CBHW071945170626
46813CB00005B/1833